The Aader

To: K K Lee

The Aader

Brian B. Wong

iUniverse, Inc.
New York Lincoln Shanghai

The Aader

iUniverse books may be ordered through booksellers or by contacting:

iUniverse
2021 Pine Lake Road, Suite 100
Lincoln, NE 68512
www.iuniverse.com
1-800-Authors (1-800-288-4677)

ISBN-13: 978-0-595-36910-2 (pbk)
ISBN-13: 978-0-595-81322-3 (ebk)
ISBN-10: 0-595-36910-3 (pbk)
ISBN-10: 0-595-81322-4 (ebk)

Printed in the United States of America

This book is dedicated to my mother, for her artistic assistance, and to my father, for his endless encouragement. This book is also dedicated to my sister, Erin, for the initial proofreading and for being the best sister in the world.

Introduction

As the Navarian Army trickled down the path, dark clouds began to cover the skies. A sorcerer carefully placed bottles of black liquid into a small building and cast a spell so that only the rightful person, or people, would be able to find them. He then ran back into the castle and up the stairs to the wing turret. He found the king sitting on his regal throne and staring out his window at the vast army.

"King Oaks, I have hidden the liquids. The Navarians will not be able to find them," he said humbly.

"I have known you for my entire life, ever since you came with me to build this kingdom. Now, Relvin Yardes of the Four Kingdoms, I give you the amulet," the king said in a deep, husky voice.

Hearing the king's words, an elf scampered to a shelf and opened a steel box. He took out the amber stone and handed it to Relvin. Its incomparable smoothness surpassed any other stone the baron had ever seen. It caught a rare ray of autumn sunlight and reflected specks of blinding light across the dull room.

Led by King Oaks, the Four Kingdoms Army marched out. Behind the king and two rows of swordsmen were the three barons who had helped start the Four Kingdoms. King Oaks broke into a sudden run, leading his army toward the Navarians. He recognized the man in front as Chief Arven II. They had always been mortal enemies. The king raised his hand and flourished his sword. Hundreds of arrows shot from the king's army, striking the unaware Navarian archers. While his people hid under their round shields, he ran forward and thrust his sword toward his archnemesis. Around him, his army advanced, shooting arrows and eagerly picking sword fights with their enemies. Occasionally, a frustrated Navarian would yell a fierce war cry and throw his axe high up into the air. Most of the time, the scene would end with a dead Navarian. "Navar!" someone yelled. Light shot out from the mass of King Oak's army toward Chief Arven. The Navarian chief was engulfed in a cloud of darkness. When the smoke cleared, a few Navarians lay dead, yet Arven somehow remained on his feet.

Dragons began swooping toward the armies like hawks to mice. They killed everyone they could, for dragons were once a wild breed of animals. King Oaks threw one of his jewels up at a dragon. "Barons!" he yelled. Immediately, his friends ran from their respective battles to protect their king. The dragon he had thrown the jewel at swooped down and grabbed it in his mouth. It halted inches above the ground, reaching its sharp talons out toward King Oaks. The king ran around the side of the monster and jumped onto the dragon. The great beast stopped for a moment, seemingly confused by the king's presence, but soon resumed its killing spree. Whenever the dragon swooped toward one of his own people, the king slapped his legs against the dragon and forced it to change direction. Some of the braver of his knights followed suit, and soon many were up in the air. And thus King Oaks began the tradition of training dragons.

Chapter 1

Far away, beyond where any of your friends have gone, lies Pey-dran. If you were to go there, it would look like the human world, *our* world, way back when there were castles, dragons, kings, queens…you know the rest. But anybody who lived there long enough would realize there were many differences from our world.

Our story begins in a region of Peydran known as Dragondaire. It was nearing the most dreaded time of the year, when the tax collectors made their rounds, collecting payment from every farmer in Dragondaire and Grutch, so that nearly every farming family had to work ten times harder in order to have what they needed to survive. The tax collectors collected money every year and deposited the proceeds into the Taxes Bank, which was hidden deep inside Grutch and guarded heavily. The collection money was used by the Grutch scholars to test out new ideas and inventions, which barely ever worked.

Aaden Oaks, a boy of sixteen, lived with his older brother, Freddy, and his father, Orcher, outside of Dragondaire. The advantage of this was that it took the tax collectors longer to find them, giving them more time to get the money they needed. The downside of the location was that native animals, such as foxes and wolves, often ravaged the family's crops.

Aaden could be considered slightly tall for his age. His black hair usually resembled a tangled mop that fell into his green eyes. His extreme slimness often led neighbors to remark that he wasn't eating enough, which was true. It was said that he got most of his looks from his mother, who had died of a fever about a year before.

Aaden's family owned two acres of farmland that was filled with all kinds of vegetables and surrounded a small four-room wooden cabin that they had built with money borrowed from Orcher's uncle, Oodan.

Now Oodan, on the other hand, lived in Farmlinder, a prosperous valley where the soil was rich and plants grew quickly and the produce tasted best. Farmlinder was very small, located between Dragondaire and Grutch. Land there was scarcely populated, for the land was very, very expensive. Oodan's large one-story house and single barn were surrounded by about three acres of land, which he maintained well with help from Aaden, who visited him every once in a while. In return, Oodan would lend the Oaks money when they needed it, and sometimes he loaned them supplies. The Oaks knew that Oodan didn't really need their help, for he could hire people anywhere. But he found odd tasks that needed to be done especially for Aaden Oaks.

Since tax time was approaching, Aaden was sent to Oodan's barn more often than usual, while Freddy watered and planted vegetables and Orcher hunted animals around their own cabin. This was how things usually went, but sometimes, when Oodan didn't need help, Aaden took half of the responsibility for the crops.

Periodically, Aaden and Freddy were sent into Dragondaire, pulling a homemade wagon full of vegetables (especially cabbages) to sell. They were not valued very highly and could only be traded for small things, like wooden boxes or small pieces of shiny rock. Sometimes it took hours for the two to find people willing to buy their vegetables. Even so, Orcher told them before every trip, "Come back with nothing but the shiny coins we rightfully deserve!" Sometimes, though, the brothers bought impractical items, such as pieces of candy or strings of yarn, without their father's knowledge or approval.

Oodan had a different way of selling his vegetables. He sent for a merchant to drive a wagon to his house, loaded up the vegetables, gave Oodan the payment, and then took the food to the king. Only the nobility ate the food from Farmlinder, which explained Oodan's wealth. He came to Farmlinder early and invested all of his money in his land. He made more and more of a profit each year by selling his food exclusively to the prestigious.

Early one morning Aaden and Freddy took their wagon into Dragondaire, only two weeks before the tax collectors were to arrive.

"We'd better not buy anything," Freddy said.

"Hey, you're the one who always buys things, anyway!" Aaden retorted.

"What about all of the times when you bought those...red twisty things?" Freddy said. He pulled the wagon away from Aaden in front of a merchant. Before Aaden could respond, Freddy asked, "Vegetables?"

"Don't buy, just sell," the merchant replied. So the two continued their search for a willing customer.

It was getting late, and they still hadn't sold anything. The merchants were beginning to flip their signs so that they said CLOSED and roll their carts toward the village.

"Oh, man!" Freddy said. "Nobody's going to buy these when they can't even see them. We're going to have to get home soon. There's no point in wandering around in the dark."

"But...but it's almost tax time, and we don't have any money!" Aaden objected. He felt in his pocket. He only had two small copper coins, and that was his life savings. "The king might buy them," he said.

"The king? The king? And how do you expect us to get into the castle, for crying out loud?" Freddy exploded. Aaden knew his questions were rhetorical ones.

Aaden ran up to a merchant who was just pulling his cart away. "Sir, would you like to buy some vegetables? They're only one copper coin for...a lot."

"I'll buy two heads of cabbage, but that's it!" the merchant said. Freddy, with a surprised smile on his face, stuck his hands into the wagon and brought the man two heads of cabbage.

"Here you go. Keep the tip." The man took the cabbages and placed one copper coin in Freddy's hand. Aaden was stunned. He could have gotten ten cabbages for a copper coin! The merchant walked away with a smile on his face.

"Come on, let's go back." Freddy said, stuffing the money in his pocket. He grabbed the cart and Aaden, and they ran back to the house.

Back at the house, Orcher angrily looked at Freddy. "Why so many vegetables?" he boomed. "You must have sold—let me think—*none!*"

Freddy stepped back, then handed his father the copper coin from his pocket.

"Tomorrow, you will go back," Orcher said, his tone less menacing now that he had copper in his hands. "And you will sell them all. Aaden, if we don't have enough money, I will use yours." Aaden saw that he was serious and automatically stuck his right hand into his pocket to feel his coins.

"Now, go back to your room and stay there." Orcher threw Aaden and Freddy one carrot each and turned around.

In his room, Aaden looked around. His small one-log desk was covered with things that he had found when farming: odd rocks, long weeds, feathers, and even a sharp tooth he had found long ago, probably from a wolf. On the floor was one deerskin rug, which covered the rough, splintery wood that made up his room.

There was a box on a shelf, neatly cut and very heavy, that Aaden had found sitting in between two branches of a tree in the Northern Woods. He could never get it open, for there was a lock hole carved into it, but he always dreamed of a life savings of treasure hidden inside. His brother wanted it very badly, but Aaden would never give it up.

Freddy slept in the room next to Aaden's, next to the living room, next to Orcher's room. He constantly barged into Aaden's room when Aaden wasn't there and rummaged around, looking for something interesting. That was how he had found the box.

Today was like any other day: Aaden and Freddy were sent to their rooms to lie down on their straw beds, with only a vegetable or two for supper. Every once in a while, Freddy would sneak into Aaden's room and check to see if he was sleeping.

"What do you want?" Aaden could hear Freddy's footsteps closing in on his room.

Freddy tiptoed forward. "Shhhh!" he whispered. "Don't wake Dad!" Freddy walked to Aaden's box and lifted it above his head, searching for a secret opening.

"Hey, put it back," Aaden said, his eyes wide open. Freddy shook the box slightly but heard nothing. "It's empty."

"No, it's not." Aaden said firmly. Freddy walked over to Aaden's bed and picked up the knife that Aaden always slept with, just in case.

"Don't!" Aaden tried to hit the knife out of Freddy's hand, but he had already jumped away. Before Aaden could get off his bed, Freddy had already begun slicing the top off the box. Aaden knew it was pointless to fight now.

Freddy threw off the top of the box and stuck his head inside. "What in the...?" He pulled out a green piece of wood that was covered on all sides with glass. Inside were four very large gold coins, in the corners, and one gigantic gold coin in the center. Aaden knew the coins were in mint condition from their brilliant shine.

Stamped into the coins were pictures of the kings of Grutch, Dragondaire, Ciliagus, and one other person whom Aaden didn't recognize. Freddy jumped up and started running toward the door.

"No!" Aaden yelled. Heavy footsteps could be heard outside. Aaden jumped off his bed and snatched the case from Freddy as he ran for his room. Aaden threw the case under his bed and jumped into the straw.

"What are you doing back there?" Orcher boomed. Aaden pretended that he was waking up.

"Is it morning…already?" he murmured. Orcher walked into his room.

"Go back to sleep!" he yelled before going back out the door.

In the morning, when Aaden peeked under his bed, he found nothing but his copper coins—his life savings. He looked around his room, but saw no traces of robbery. He got up out of bed and walked down the hall into Freddy's room.

"Freddy, where'd you put the case?" he asked. Freddy rubbed his eyes wearily and looked at Aaden.

"I don't have it. You don't either?" Freddy said. When he saw that Aaden didn't believe what he heard, he said, "I swear. I didn't."

"Well, then, who did?" Aaden asked.

"How would I know? Maybe Dad did," Freddy said. "But you can't ask him, because if he didn't, then he'll be mad because you didn't tell him."

Aaden walked down the hallway and peeked into Orcher's room. His father was sleeping there, snoring loudly. He tiptoed through the living room to the front door. He opened it and sprinted outside, closing the door. He knew that without the gold, his family would not be able to survive tax time. But maybe they would if he wasn't there.

Aaden was tired of living the life of an average, poor farm boy. He hated waking up at five in the morning just to pick weeds and help Oodan. He was tired of eating barely anything and being yelled at every day by his father. He was tired of being pushed around by Freddy. He was tired of being poor! He made his decision and headed away from his house at a rapid rate.

Walking up to a slightly larger house than his own, located near the castle of Dragondaire, he knocked four times slow, then three times fast. Within moments, the door swung open to reveal his best friend, Rederin.

"Can I talk to you alone?" Aaden asked. In response, Rederin called out, "Mom, I'm going to talk to Aaden for a moment."

"Okay, Rederin," a voice called from inside. Rederin walked outside and closed the door.

"Rederin, aren't you tired of living an average life? Barely making it?" Aaden asked.

Rederin thought a moment. "Yeah, I guess," he said.

"Me too. I know my family won't be able to survive tax time. So how about me and you and the rest of the guys go on a quest?" Aaden said. He had been friends with Faten, Drakint, Cedar, and Rederin since they all had attended the one-room schoolhouse in the village.

"Sounds exciting, but what kind of a quest?" Rederin asked. He looked excited.

"How about...we hunt for dragonstones! Remember how we dreamed of this when we were in school?" Aaden said.

"But how, and when, and where?" Rederin said.

"Tomorrow, seven o' clock, the Northern Woods, the clearing with the stream running through the middle. You can tell Drakint and I'll tell Faten and Cedar," Aaden replied.

"Can't wait. I'll miss my parents though," Rederin said.

"Me too. Oh, and tell Drakint to bring his money." And with that, Aaden was off, sprinting to Faten and Cedar's house. They were brothers he'd known all his life, since their mom and his dad were cousins. They had always gotten along well and shared the same interests. Faten was younger than the others and tended to follow them around. As it turned out, Aaden almost ran into the two as he rounded a bend in the road. They had been on their way to see him. Cedar and Faten were as fed up with the lack of opportunity and adventure in their lives as Aaden was and it didn't take long to convince them to go on a quest. After all, they had planned such an adventure for years, just waiting for the right moment. After agreeing on the time and meeting place, Aaden hurried back home to prepare. He hoped he would be able to get there and back home before Orcher woke up.

"Don't just stand there, Aaden. Are you just going to stand there or are you going to go gather firewood?" boomed his father, Orcher.

"Gather firewood, Father. Just one moment," Aaden replied, trying to conceal his excitement, none of which was due to the firewood or his father.

He raced to his small room and picked up a bag from under his bed.

"Oi, where are you off to, Aaden? And who's that money for?" Freddy asked, walking into Aaden's room.

"You may be my older brother, Fred, but some things I keep secret," Aaden replied.

And with that, he ran out the back door into the wood as fast as he could muster while lugging his axe behind him.

After about an hour of running, Aaden found himself in a large clearing with a small stream running through it. He stopped and took a look at his timepiece, which he carried around his neck.

Just in time for the meeting, he thought to himself. After a few minutes, Aaden could make out the figure of his best friend, Rederin, running toward him.

"Aaden! I just barely made it past my mom." Rederin's parents were more protective than Aaden's father.

"I'm just glad you made it. Have you heard from any of the others?"

"Not yet."

"Look! I think I see Faten and Cedar coming."

"Oh, yeah, you're right."

"Aaden! And who's with you? Oh, it's Rederin!" Faten yelled, coming closer. He was out of breath and visibly excited.

"Did you bring your money with you?" Rederin asked when Faten and Cedar reached the clearing.

"Wouldn't leave without it," Cedar said for both of them, pulling out a sack of coins and shaking it.

"Gotcha!" a short blond haired teen yelled as he jumped from behind a boulder and snatched away the coins in mid-jingle. It was the final member of their group, Drakint, who tended to be more competitive than the other friends, and sometimes had a sharp tongue.

"Oi! Drakint, you scared me," Cedar said, grabbing back his sack.

"Well, looks like we got the whole crew now," Aaden said.

"Now all's we need is a captain or some sort of leader," Rederin said.

"I nominate Rederin," Aaden said.

"I nominate Aaden," Cedar said.

"I second the nomination," said Faten.

"I third the nomination," Rederin said.

"Well, then, that's final. Aaden is our leader," Drakint said.

"Okay," Aaden said. "Let's head to Oodan's barn and see if he'll let us work there, so we can save money to buy what we need. Any objections?"

No one said anything, and so the group began the long walk through the Northern Woods toward Farmlinder, where Oodan lived.

That night, when Aaden was on the brink of falling asleep, he heard footsteps. Knowing he would be no match for an adult, he pretended to be asleep. The person bent down with his head nearly level with Aaden's, facing Rederin. As he looked closely, Aaden could tell it was Drakint. Aaden heard the soft rustling of coins jingling, and then Drakint went back to bed.

When Aaden woke up, he felt confused. *Should I tell Rederin? Was I just dreaming?* he kept thinking to himself. Eventually these thoughts exited his mind as he returned to his fantasy dream world of flying dragons and pots of gold.

"Rederin! Wake up!" he yelled. "Come on, guys!"

Soon the whole gang was back up and on the move. By noon Oodan's red barn was visible. Without realizing it, they started walking faster until finally breaking into a run. By now the axe Aaden was carrying felt much heavier, and he couldn't keep his mind from drifting back to the pain it was causing him. About to ask Rederin if he could carry it, Aaden looked up and saw that they were only about ten yards away from Oodan's porch. Rederin knocked on the door four times.

"Aaden! Hello," Oodan said, opening the door wide. "What brings you here this fine day?"

"We were wondering if you needed some help around the barn. You see—"

Oodan interrupted, saying, "Before you say more, why don't you come inside? I'll prepare some tea." He moved out of the doorway. Aaden and his group walked over to a green couch in front of a coffee table and sat down. Aaden leaned his axe against his black chair.

"Well, then, what were you saying, dear boy?" the farmer asked, putting a kettle over the fire.

"Well, you see, we're on a quest to travel across the world and acquire dragonstones. But unfortunately for us, we have no experience and only a little money. That is why we want to work for you, sir."

"I'll tell you what, young lads. Three of you can gather firewood and two of you can pick weeds and water the crops. For each hour of work, you will get two copper coins for the whole group. I will also give you the food and water you need," Oodan said.

"I accept the deal that you offer us, sir, as long as we all agree." Aaden was still too young to realize the extent of Oodan's generosity. "Crewmembers, if you think this is a good idea, say aye."

"Aye!" came the voices of the crew.

"When shall we start work, Oodan?" Aaden asked.

"Right now, I suppose. Who would like to chop wood today?" the farmer asked, taking a sip of tea.

"I'll do it," Aaden said.

"Me too," Rederin said.

"I guess I'll do it," Drakint said.

"Well, then, here are two more axes for you two. And there's a wagon for the wood over there," Oodan said, handing the two boys axes and pointing at a large wooden wagon in the corner of the room.

It was late in the afternoon and Aaden was about to ask his friends whether they should head back to the barn when he heard a loud noise that was a mixture of a screech, a growl, and a howl. "Did you hear that?" he asked.

"Uh huh," Drakint said.

"What do you think it is, Aaden?" Rederin asked.

"I don't know, but I think we should run back to the barn. It could be dangerous."

"I agree," Rederin said.

"One, two, three, *run!*" Drakint said. Immediately the boys dropped their axes in the wagon, grabbed the handle, and ran.

When they got to the barn, they threw open the back door, panting.

"Oodan!" they yelled together.

"What?" Oodan said, emerging from the living room.

"We heard an odd screeching noise when we were in the wood. We thought it might be something dangerous, so we ran back here," Drakint said, gasping for air.

"Well, boys, first of all, I have no idea what you heard. It even might have been a dragon; who knows? I was hoping you might get more wood than this, but since you're already back, why don't you go fetch the other two, and I'll pay you for your work."

"Cedar!" Aaden yelled when they were in talking distance of the field where Cedar was working.

"Yeah?"

"We're done working for the day. Can you get Faten and meet us in the barn?" Rederin said.

"Okay! I'll be there in a minute!"

Aaden watched as Cedar darted across the field and came back with his brother.

"We heard a growl in the wood and we turned back," Aaden said. "Anything exciting happen to you?"

"Nothing much," Faten said as they walked toward the barn. "So are we going to keep the same jobs tomorrow? Or should we switch?"

When they reached the barn, Oodan said, "I am going to put the seven coins I owe you into this sack."

Aaden remembered watching Drakint take some money from Rederin and realized that pooling their money would solve the problem completely.

"I think we should pool our money," he said, pulling out his coins and dumping the money into the larger sack. The rest of his crew members did the same, and Drakint took the longest time about it.

Surprise

Surprise, surprise
You find what you don't expect—
Open the door, but find the porch
Empty,
Flip through a book, and find
That it's blank,
Begin the descent
Of a scary
Rollercoaster:
Surprise, surprise,
Always a surprise.

Chapter 2

"I'm going to pick weeds on the other side, okay?" Aaden said.

"Okay. We'll switch posts later," Rederin replied.

Walking to the other side, Aaden saw a dark blue rock in the corner of the farm under a prickly bush. At first Aaden just ignored it and continued pulling weeds, but then he decided to check it out. *Just for a moment. What harm can come to me?* he thought to himself, heading for the bush. When he reached it, he rolled up his sleeve and shoved his arm under it. At first all he felt was sticky brown mud, but moments later he felt something hard. "Ow!" he yelled. The moment he touched it, an icy pain ran through his fingertips all the way up to his shoulder.

Under different circumstances he would have gone back to the barn and asked Oodan for some ointment, but then Oodan would start asking him questions. Instead, he just sat there for a few minutes, staring at the rock. When the pain finally subsided, he looked on his arm for a scratch or some other injury. To his astonishment, he saw a blue *X* on the underside of his wrist. It was the exact same color as the rock.

Deciding to forget about the mysterious rock, Aaden went back to his job for a few hours. After he had switched posts with Rederin and the sun was beginning to set, he decided to try touching the rock once more.

This time, nothing unusual happened. Thinking that its magic only appeared when somebody touched it for the first time, he stuffed it into his pocket and continued working. About an hour later, Oodan called them in for supper.

Everyone was seated at a large wooden table in the room next to the living room. On the table were heaping plates filled with mashed potatoes, red and black berries, and pieces of loose meat and drumsticks.

"I imagine vegetable prices have risen," Aaden said, remembering the time many months ago when he and his family had gone to Oodan to buy some food.

"You'd better believe it!" Oodan said, grabbing a piece of meat from the plate in the middle.

When he got into bed, Aaden had a very tough time going to sleep. He kept wondering about the rock he had found earlier. Later that night, he heard a soft cracking sound. At first there was a crack every few minutes, but as time passed, the cracking noise became more constant. As dawn approached, Aaden had a splitting headache and had slept very little.

He went to the main room and looked into the sack. Covering the top was a note, which read

Aaden, you and your friends have done very well,
but now is your time to depart and continue your journey.
Take all the food you need from my larder.
I wish you all the best.

Aaden picked up the note and looked into the sack. Sure enough, it was filled almost to the top with coins, and there was a rope atop it. He ran down the hall to where Rederin was sleeping and opened the door.

"Rederin! Wake up!"

"What's up?"

"The sack of copper is full. Now we can begin our journey!"

"Really?"

"Really. Let's wake everyone." Aaden rushed back into his room and stuffed the blue rock into his pocket, then he went to join his friends.

"Seeing as how we're about to embark on our journey, do you think we should have a name?" Faten said.

"How about the Dragonhunters?" Drakint said.

"What about the Aader?" asked Faten.

"I like that name," Rederin said.

"Me too," Cedar said.

"It beats the Dragonhunters," said Drakint.

"As the leader, I declare Aader our official name," Aaden said. "Before we do anything else, I think we should make a cabin somewhere in the wood." And so the Aader set out on their adventure.

It was midday when the Aader stopped near an apple tree for a small meal. They all sat down and began eating apples. Aaden noticed a sudden flash of light and the swift movement of a black-cloaked figure off to their left. When he turned to look, the figure had disappeared into the trees, and Rederin had fallen over and lay motionless.

"Rederin!" Aaden yelled frantically. He bent down and put his hand on Rederin's chest. Nothing. But wait—there it was again, the faint thumping of a heart, in between long moments of stillness. "We have to take him to the oracle! Now! He is dying. That must have been an evil sorcerer. He must have put a spell on the apple and poisoned him." His last words were accompanied by tears. "How can Rederin die?"

Aaden pulled himself up from the ground. "Come on. We must go north to find the oracle. He might save Rederin." Faten and Cedar moved in and picked up Rederin, then they all started walking north, deeper and deeper into the wood. After a while, Aaden felt as though they were being watched. Every few minutes he would quickly turn his head to the side and check to make sure they were not being followed.

"Hey guys, do you feel like you're being watched?" he said.

"Nope," the rest of the crew replied. Sometimes Aader wished he could be as carefree as his friends.

Aaden felt a rustling in the pocket where he had put his blue rock. When he looked down, he was astounded to see a blue head peeping at him through a crack in the rock. "Uh...guys? I think I have a dragon egg."

"What did you say?" Faten asked.

"I think I have a dragon egg."

"Where?" Drakint said, bewildered.

"Here," Aaden said, pulling the blue egg from his pocket and showing it to his friends, who immediately crowded around excitedly and started asking questions. Dragon eggs were very hard to come by, and they could hardly believe he had found one. "I found it on the farm and I thought it was just a rock, until now."

By this time the dragon's body was already halfway out, revealing two small, dark blue wings. Realizing that if he kept holding the egg out the dragon would fall, Aaden sat on the mossy ground and put the egg on his lap. Moments later, the dragon had completely climbed out of the egg and onto Aaden's shoulder, falling instantly into a deep sleep. From head to tail, the dragon measured about one foot long.

As excited as they were about seeing the baby dragon, the boys knew they had to get help for their friend, so they hurried onward. As they walked, Aaden kept thinking about a good name for his dragon. Occasionally, when he thought of a name he liked, he whispered it out loud. Every time he did so, his dragon shook its head in disapproval. "What about Harlume?" Aaden looked at his dragon and he could tell it was thinking. Suddenly, the dragon shot out a tiny ball of flame that disappeared soon after appearing. Aaden took the outburst as a sign of his dragon's approval.

A few minutes later, when the Aader were in a clearing, Aaden spotted a giant city between some trees. *We must have reached the other side of the woods already,* Aaden thought. By this time it was late in the afternoon and everybody was starting to get sleepy.

"Do you think we should camp here and get a good night's rest before we go see if the kingdom of Grutch has some horses we can use to find the oracle?" Cedar suggested.

"Sounds like a fine plan to me," Aaden said.

"Are we going to set up a tent or something?" Drakint said.

Just then Aaden felt a tingling in his shoulder. He turned his head and saw his baby dragon yawning. He pulled out his sack of gold.

"Hey, Faten, could you keep my coins in your sack for the night? I was thinking about putting my dragon, Harlume, into my sack," Aaden asked.

"Sure," Faten replied, emptying the coins into his sack and closing it.

"Thanks," Aaden said before opening his bag, putting Harlume inside, and closing it.

Almost immediately after lying down and closing his eyes, Aaden's mind went blank and he began dreaming.

> *A boy ran nearer to the red dragon, yet remained in hiding. Finally, the dragon breathed fire that scorched the earth's surface and created a valuable dragonstone. All of a sudden, the dragon swooped up and disappeared into the emptiness above. A sorcerer jumped out from behind a tree and dove for the precious stone, covering it with dragonskin, which would save the dragonstone from disappearing. Out of nowhere, the dragon reappeared and threw a fatal fireball at the sorcerer. The dragonstone was hovering in midair, about to disappear, when the boy jumped from his post and covered the stone with dragonskin. The dragon threw a fireball at him too, but he dodged just in time. He ran as fast as he could into the wood until he was aware that people were following him. Arrows followed him but he ducked quickly. He continued running until he felt an arrow pierce his skin.*

Aaden awoke from his odd dream feeling sore and very shaky. To his surprise, his friends were wide awake and picking berries. He wondered how long he had been sleeping.

"Aaden, you're awake. What were you dreaming about?" Cedar asked once he saw that Aaden was awake.

"It was nothing. Why?"

"Don't you know? You kept squirming and shaking the whole night."

"Come and help us pick berries, Aaden," Drakint said.

Chapter 3

"Hello. We've come in search of horses," Aaden said to the guard.

"Enjoy your stay," the guard grunted, hauling open the stone gates.

"Wow," Cedar said, "this place is nice." Everywhere they looked they saw magnificent towers made of silver and gold, giant stone houses, and tons of people crowding the streets. In the middle of the city was a castle higher than the highest towers and bigger than the biggest houses.

"The fastest horses are probably kept in the castle stable, so I guess we should start there," Aaden said.

When they got near the castle, they saw a woman and asked her for directions.

"Oh, yes. Go to the corner and turn right. It shouldn't take you too long to find it. What happened to the boy you're carrying?"

"We're not exactly sure what happened. He just ate an apple and fainted. Thanks for your help."

They hurried on and entered the stables to find a bearded man sitting behind a large desk.

"We would like to purchase five horses for our journey. We need to get to our destination quickly, for our friend's life is on the line," Aaden found himself shouting to the stable foreman.

"Five horses will cost six hundred and fifty-four gold coins," the man said.

"Would this be enough, sir?" Aaden put the sack of coins on the counter.

"I'm afraid that will not be nearly enough. But if you'd like, I'd be happy to trade five horses for that dragon of yours," the man said with a gleam in his eye, looking at Harlume, who rode atop Aaden's shoulder.

"No, thank you. Do you know of any other places that sell horses around here?"

"Not in this city, but there are some further off."

"Thank you for your time, sir." The five friends left the barn and went into the open street.

"Are you ready to steal some horses?" Cedar asked.

"How are we supposed to steal horses right outside the castle, when there are people all around?" Faten said.

"I thought you'd never ask," Cedar began. "Well, you see, I've visited here several times with my father and brother, and I even helped out one summer. Every day, the horses are taken out of the barn for cleaning. The first step is to find the men who clean and take their clothes, so everybody has a special suit. Then we will go back into the barn and take the horses outside the cleaning room. Next, we take off our suits and ride away, leaving everyone to think that we bought the horses. According to the schedule I saw on the desk in the barn, one of the cleaners should pass by this garbage can every ten minutes. So if we just hide behind the can for fifty minutes, we'll get our suits. I know what you're thinking: 'Where are we going to put Rederin?' When we go in to get the horses, we will have to pretend that he is normal and just have him take a horse. Yes, he will be in a suit too."

The others were all amazed that Cedar could remember all this and come up with such a complicated and dangerous plan. Since they needed the horses and they needed them fast, they quickly hid behind the garbage can and waited.

"Look over there. I think I see one coming," Faten whispered, moving his head toward the left.

"Ready...and...*jump!*" Aaden yelled. At his cue, Faten and Cedar jumped out from behind the can, grabbed the man, and pulled him back behind the trash can.

"What are you doing to me?" the man demanded.

"Uh...well..." Faten said slowly.

"We were wondering if we could do your job for today. Uh...we really like horses...a lot," Aaden said.

"Sure," the man said cheerfully. "But why did you have to grab me and hide me behind a trash can?"

"We...uh...didn't want to attract that much attention," Aaden said.

"Here, let me take off my suit," the cleaner said, removing his jacket and pulling off his hat.

"Listen, do you think you could tell the other cleaners that there are four people that can do the cleaning today? They just have to come here," Cedar said.

"Okay. Thanks for doing my job."

"Anytime."

After about ten minutes, four men came walking down the street toward the garbage can, carrying cleaners' suits in their arms.

"Are you the cleaning substitutes?"

"Right you are," Cedar said.

"You can just leave your suits here and we'll do your job," Aaden said.

The men handed their suits to the Aader, then walked away with smiles on their faces. The friends put on the suits and walked toward the barn. Aaden put his dragon in his pocket so as not to attract too much attention. They arrived at the stable.

"Hello. We have all decided to work together today," Aaden said to the stableman.

"But what about all of the other horses?"

"More of the cleaners will come later." The Aader walked over to the horses, took four of the black stallions, and then walked toward the exit.

"Hang on!" the stableman yelled.

"Run!" Aaden screamed. The Aader leaped onto their horses and galloped away. Drakint held Rederin; Faten carried the bag of coins.

"Fakes!" the shopkeeper yelled. But it was too late: the Aader were already out of sight.

They happily galloped toward the oracle. Little did they know that the stableman was reporting the news to the king and queen, and now all of Grutch would be after them.

"We should probably take off our suits before we go any further. If they're chasing us, we'll be less likely to be noticed that way," Aaden said. They slowed their horses, dismounted, and took off the suits. They hid the suits in some bushes, then got back on their horses and galloped away.

They rode quickly for a while, then slowed their pace early in the afternoon. Aaden pulled Harlume from his pocket and rested him on his shoulder. It had only been one day since his dragon had been born, but it had already grown about an inch, and it was bulging out of his pocket. Every once in a while, Harlume would spit out a fireball. Each new fireball was bigger than the last.

"Is that the oracle you were talking about, Aaden?" Cedar said, pointing at a cabin between two trees.

"I think so," Aaden replied. "But there's only one way to find out."

As they got closer to the cabin, they saw smoke rising from the chimney in rings. Birds merrily chirped around an apple tree next to the house.

Aaden knocked twice and waited. An old man came to the door. His hair was gray and his face was bony, but his piercing eyes made him look very vibrant and alive.

"Hello there, young lads. What brings you to my humble abode, and what has happened to the dead one?" the oracle said slowly.

"You see, our friend ate an apple and immediately fell to the ground. His heart is beating, but we're not sure how much longer he'll be able to hold on. We came to you to see if you could help him," Aaden said.

"Let me think." The oracle closed his eyes and nodded. "Well, I could help him, but I'm afraid one of the most important ingredients of the medicine is extremely rare and I just used the last bit I had on a merchant. It is called pickled willow bark, and it only grows on young, green trees. If you are that determined to save your friend, you can go look for some in the deepest part of the woods, for I am too old to hunt for it myself."

"Anything for Rederin, sir. Do you think you could keep him and our belongings in your house while we are searching?" Aaden said.

"Sure. Just put them in the back there, and you can be on your way." Aaden and the oracle hauled Rederin and their belongings into the house.

"The most likely place to find pickled willow trees is near the upper Northern Woods River. If you keep going east, you will get there. Farewell, my young friends, and good luck finding the pickled willow bark!" the oracle yelled as the Aader galloped off.

"I don't like the look of this place, guys. Are you sure we're going the right way?" Drakint asked, looking around at the blackness. Occasionally they glimpsed two shiny eyes.

"I don't know, Drakint, but I think we should probably go to sleep. It's getting dark," Aaden said.

"Aah!" Drakint suddenly yelled.

"What, Draki—Ow!" Aaden screamed.

"Something's got us!" everybody yelled.

"We've got you!" a deep voice boomed.

"You're coming with us, you little horse-stealers," said a second voice. "You're going to jail, pipsqueaks. You thought you could steal from the kingdom of Grutch and get away with it? Crazy kids." Then the man punched Aaden in the eye and knocked him out.

~   ~   ~

"Where am I?" Aaden found himself in a small stone room, lying on a stone bench and staring at a stone ceiling. On one side of the room there were iron bars trapping him inside. "Harlume, where are you?" he said in a dreamy daze. Something tickled his back and Aaden turned around to see Harlume, a whole foot bigger. His wings were the length of two pencils put together.

All of a sudden a tray was passed through a flap near the iron bars. It held cold soup and a pitcher of water. Aaden realized how dry his throat was, and took a mouthful of soup. "Yuck!" It tasted horrible. He grabbed the pitcher of water and drank some. His mind went blank.

He woke up an hour later, feeling sour and confused. "Why did I blank out again?" he said. Harlume touched the pitcher of water with her wing, as if in answer to Aaden's question. "Oh yeah, I remember. I drank some water and then blanked out. They must have put some spell on it or something to keep me from escaping. *Ervin wak!*" Aaden cursed, staring at the iron bars.

A small fireball hit the bars and then disappeared as quickly as it had come. Just then, the blue *X* on Aaden's wrist started hurting. It shone red for a split second before returning to its normal color.

"Wow! Did you just see that, Harlume? I made fire from a curse word!" Harlume nodded. "Let me try another curse word. *Vater wret!*" Aaden yelled, still staring at the iron bars. All of a sudden, a large piece of ice hit one of the bars, and once again the *X* on Aaden's wrist stung and then shone red. "Magic! I can do magic!" Aaden decided to say the worst curse word he knew. His parents had forbidden him to ever say it, but this was a whole different case.

"*Darder wan!*" Immediately a blue light enclosed the iron bars. Boom! All of the bars broke at once. "Wow! Well, I was hoping to stay here until I mastered magic, but since the bars are already broken, let's go!" Aaden yelled.

Aaden scooped up Harlume as he ran toward the front door. "*Ervin wak!*" Aaden yelled while staring at the two guards. Two fireballs, bigger than the first one, rushed out of his mind and hit the guards right in the center of their chests, knocking them out.

Aaden ran toward the open door and rushed outside. Everyone stared at him. He ran past the crowds as fast as he could, dodging the knights and guards of the city until he entered a small wood. Guards continually shot arrows into the woods, but Aaden kept running for his life. Harlume was tucked safely under his arm, but he couldn't help wondering whether his friends were safe and where they were. Had they been captured too? Should he try to rescue them? Was Rederin safe with the oracle?

While Aaden was running and thinking about his friends, he didn't pay much attention to his surroundings. He was just relieved that he hadn't heard his pursuers in a while. But then he noticed that there were no longer any trees around him, and there was sand at his feet. Aaden froze. He was standing on the outskirts of the burning-hot Halder Desert. There was no escaping it. It stretched on for miles and miles in every direction except south, where the prison was. It was covered with *dunlops,* bubbling pits, and screechers. The first step onto the Halder Desert was very hard to take, for once you began walking the Halder, there would be no turning back. Only a few people had managed to cross the Halder by foot, and those were full-grown men with supplies and plenty of water. But Aaden knew it was a risk he would have to take.

The sand of the Halder was like no sand you might see on the beach of a bay or an ocean. The sand of the Halder was sucking mush that made it hard even to pick up one's foot once it was down, and there was no water to be found.

As you might have guessed, it was tough for Aaden to take his first step onto the legendary desert, but eventually he set out on his journey across the Halder. The first day of walking was the easiest for Aaden, and he thought that the journey might not be so hard after all. But then came the matter of sleeping. He decided to take a chance and lie down by a bubbling pit, for the day had tired him out so much that it was hard to move.

When he woke up, Aaden felt horrible. His throat was very dry and he could barely manage to talk. Then he had an idea. "*Vater wret!*" he yelled, using the last of his energy. A piece of ice fell into his lap. He picked it up and ate it. It tasted better than anything else he had ever tasted in his entire life. With new energy and a new plan, Aaden continued on his way, conjuring up a piece of ice whenever he got thirsty or really hot.

He looked up and saw the figure of a large castle far ahead of him. The next moment it wasn't there. *Very odd,* he thought.

As Aaden kept walking, he noticed the castle appearing and then disappearing more and more. He couldn't take his eyes off of it. The farther he walked, the bigger it got. Curious, he began walking faster and faster until he was near the end of the Halder Desert.

To his surprise, where the castle should have been, there was only air. He kept walking onward until he thought he heard footsteps or sounds off in the distance, but he didn't see anything. He realized he was not thinking very clearly and he might be imagining things. Late that night, when Aaden was lying down, he realized that there might be scouts searching for him in the desert. Suddenly, someone ran up to him.

"Aaden, Aaden! Wake up! It's me, Faten. Where were you?" Faten said joyfully.

"Faten, is that really you?"

"Of course!"

Aaden said, "I was in jail. But then I escaped and I had to go through the Halder Desert. I learned some magic, too. Where were you?"

"I was in jail too, but my jail must have been in a different location. Can you teach me some magic?"

"Well, it's really easy. All I said was 'vater wret,' and ice appeared."

Faten said, "Vater wret!" Nothing happened. "Are you sure it was 'vater wret'?"

"I think so. Let me try. Vater wret!" A piece of ice flew from Aaden's mind and hit a tree. Then his X burned and shone red.

"Wow, Aaden! What's that thing on your wrist?"

"I got it when I touched Harlume's egg. Hey, where is Harlume, anyway?"

"I think he went to catch some breakfast."

"Can he fly?"

"Oh, yeah. He's huge, too."

"Have you seen any of the other crew members?"

"Nope. You?"

"Nah ah. We should probably get going, though; I'm pretty sure the soldiers are after me," Aaden said, getting up and walking north.

"The prison I escaped from was in the north, so we probably shouldn't go there," Faten said.

"Oh yeah, you're right! I guess nobody would be looking for us in the Frosty Mountains, so we can start going that way and we might find another crew member. And I'm pretty sure Harlume will be able to find us," Aaden said.

"Okay," said Faten, and they both started walking north.

Chapter 4

"Wake up, Aaden!" Faten said loudly. "We're almost to the mountains."

"Has Harlume come back yet?" Aaden asked.

"Yeah, he's right behind you." Aaden turned his head and saw Harlume sharpening his nails on a large rock. He was now about as tall as a one-story house, and his tail was about thirty yards long.

"Are you going to ride him now?" Faten inquired. Aaden was surprised. He had heard stories in which men rode their dragons, but he had never really thought about riding Harlume.

"I...I guess," he answered. "Do you want to ride with me?"

"Oh, no thanks, I'm kind of afraid of heights."

"We should probably get going now, so we can get to the mountains as soon as possible," Aaden said, and walked up to Harlume. "I'm going to ride you today," he said softly. As if he understood, Harlume put down his paw and bent down. Aaden put one foot over Harlume's scaly back and pushed off the ground with his other foot, stabilizing himself. With three beats of his wings, the dragon rose up off the ground and into the open sky.

As Harlume began to speed up, wind rushed by Aaden's face and almost made him close his eyes. Riding the dragon was an amazing experience. To Aaden, it was like a whole different world. All of a sudden Harlume dove down, almost causing Aaden to lose his balance and fall off. His heart felt as though it had jerked up to his throat. Then there was a slight bump as Harlume landed a few yards in front of the entrance to the Frosty Mountains.

In front of them, held down by a rock, was a note flapping in the wind. Aaden dismounted, bent down, and picked it up. It read:

Aaden,
I already entered the Frosty Mountains.
Fly near the ground so you can see me.
Faten

"I wonder how he got ahead of us," Aaden said. "We must have taken a lot of time going up and down. Come on, Harlume. But this time, fly near the ground." Harlume nodded and bent down. Aaden jumped onto him and in a minute they were airborne.

"Faten! Over here!" Harlume swooped down right behind Faten.

"What took you guys so long?" Faten asked.

"I don't know. Harlume, I'm going to walk with Faten, so you can either fly above us or walk next to us." In answer, the dragon flapped its wings, waited for one moment, then flapped again and lifted off.

"Hey, Aaden, do you see that?" Faten pointed to what looked like two figures on a ridge off in the distance.

"Yeah. Do you think it's Drakint and Cedar?"

"Maybe, but we're never going to catch up to them walking."

"*We* don't need to see them to find out who they are."

Faten had a puzzled look on his face.

"Harlume!" Aaden yelled. Responding to his call, Harlume landed next to them. "See those people up there?" Harlume nodded. "Well, can you fly up there and see if they're Drakint and Cedar?" Harlume nodded, rose up, and flew toward the ridge.

In a little while, Harlume reached the figures on the ridge. The dragon pointed his wing in the direction of Aaden and Faten. The figures turned their heads and saw them. Then the two hopped onto Harlume's back and the dragon flew back. "Aaden! Faten!" Cedar yelled. "We thought we might never see you again!" Harlume landed and Drakint and Cedar climbed off.

"Why did you guys decide to come to the Frosty Mountains?" Drakint asked.

"We thought this would be the safest way to get away from those soldiers," Faten said.

Cedar asked, "Have you heard anything about there being an ancient dragonrider school or something? Aren't their secret head-quarters supposed to be deep inside the Frosty Mountains?"

"I've heard about it in legends, but I'm not sure if it's true," Aaden said.

"Come on, let's get going. *Kingdoms* are probably after us by now," Drakint said sarcastically. The group laughed out loud, not knowing how true the statement was.

All of a sudden, Harlume landed heavily in front of the group, returning from her mid-afternoon hunt. He started kicking his legs and punching the air with his wings, then pointed behind them. "Oh…my…god," they all said together. For behind them, hundreds of knights on horses were riding toward the group. Though they were actually leagues behind, riding at a normal pace, and they hadn't even noticed the group, it didn't look good to the Aader.

"Run!" yelled Aaden.

"Uh, guys, do you see what I see?" Cedar asked.

"I wish I didn't," Aaden said, near tears.

"What are you guys talking about?" Drakint asked. "The knights are still way behind us." He looked around, then added, "Never mind." The boys were in a large circle where four paths met. On all four of those paths, armies were coming after them.

"Think, guys. Keep your calm and just concentrate on a way out of here," Aaden said with some determination in his voice, wiping away his tears. The group of four started frantically pacing all about the circle, all of them staring blankly at the ground.

No one spoke until Faten broke the silence by saying, "They see us! They're coming faster! They're almost here, and we're *doomed.*"

A deep voice sounded from ahead. "And you thought you could get away with this, huh, boys?" Not one of the Aader spoke a word.

"Who are you lookin' for?" someone said from the ranks of green-clothed knights. Still, none of the group spoke.

"Speak, youngsters!" demanded a general. Nothing was heard in response.

"*Kill!*" several of the knights yelled, and then they charged.

"Help!" the Aader yelled. And then a miracle happened, and in the most unexpected way, they were saved. Aaden felt a lurch, then saw only pitch-blackness. Then Aaden and his group hit a stone floor with a crash.

"Hello," said a dwarf in front of them in a warm and welcoming voice. "Follow me."

"Um, excuse me, but who are you? Where are we, and what happened? And why? Not to be rude or anything, but you see, we were just about to be killed, and then...and then we came...here," Aaden said.

"To answer your first question, I am Dorf of the Frosty Mountains. To answer your second question, we are in the Dragonriders' Academy of Learning and Secrets," the dwarf called Dorf said as they walked down an empty stone corridor. The Aader exchanged glances of excitement. Though their heads were full of questions, they decided to wait.

"Now for your third question. A rather tricky one that is, a very tricky question. Well, you see, my job is to watch for new students for the academy. This whole choosing business starts with a thousand-year-old prophecy. The prophecy states that someone will pass through that clearing at exactly this time of day, during this particular season—someone with the true blood of a dragonrider. So when I heard the footsteps of a few young boys, I looked at my timepiece: exactly six o'clock. Then I pulled down the levers back there, and all the spaces in the clearing with extra weight fell down. Now, you probably have more questions, but now is not the right time. Right now, I am taking you to meet Dragonmaster Ponn. He is our king, our ruler. Without him, we would be nothing. And here we are: Chamber 555, reserved for our leader."

The dwarf knocked on the door five times quickly, three times slowly, then one more time. A small sheet of paper was waved from a slit on the door, then pulled back in. On cue, Dorf pulled out a small card and dropped it through the slit.

"It's Dorf, sir. No doubt about it," a prestigious voice said from inside the room.

"Let him in. I have a feeling it's important," a deeper and softer voice said. Without warning, the double doors swung open and revealed a room that looked completely different from the corridors they had walked along.

On two sides of the room, wooden staircases curved upward until they met at the second floor. Lining the perimeter of the room were many shelves filled with books. Centered between the staircases was a long mahogany desk. Behind that desk was a large chair covered with black leather. On that chair, as you might have guessed, sat Dragonmaster Ponn.

"I believe these youngsters have some dragonrider blood, sir." Dorf said.

"Oh, what a surprise! I haven't seen new dragonriders in ages. Well, then, you've done enough for now, Dorf. You can head back to your post. Elfir, you take the dragon to the dragonhouse and then meet Elvin in Room 100," the dragonmaster said. At once, the three exited the room.

"Have a seat, boys," he said, pointing to four wooden chairs that were about a foot in front of his desk. The Aader seated themselves. "First, what are your names?"

"I'm Faten."

"My name is Aaden, sir."

"Drakint."

"I'm Cedar, sir."

"And you can call me Mr. Ponn. Oh, and whenever you want, feel free to ask me questions. Here at the Dragonriders' Academy we simply train young dragonriders in the ancient arts of fighting and magic."

"Excuse me, but why is it called the Dragonriders' Academy of Learning and *Secrets*?" Drakint asked.

"A very good question. Well, in the Academy building, there are hundreds of hidden keys, all leading to secret rooms. This is because this building was used for hundreds of years by dragonriders, and back then, it was essential to have secret rooms. Over time, the keys made to open them were dropped here and there, sometimes hidden and then forgotten. We always—always—encourage our students to look for the treasures. If they find any treasure and show it to me, I'll gladly let them keep it—no questions asked. But now I have a question for you. Do any of you know any magic?"

"I know a little," Aaden said.

"Follow me," Mr. Ponn said, getting up and walking toward the staircase. The group followed him to the second story and into a small empty room made of bricks. "Show me what you know."

"*Vater wret!*" Aaden yelled, staring at one brick. All of a sudden a small piece of ice hit the brick and the *X* on Aaden's wrist glowed red. "*Ervin wak!*" A small ball of fire hit the brick. Hoping that the wall wouldn't break, Aaden yelled, "*Darder wan!*" A blue light covered the entire wall, then faded.

"Wow!" Cedar and Drakint breathed deeply. In all the excitement, he hadn't been able to tell them about his skills.

"Aaden, now that you have learned some spells, you probably think that magic is just cursing," Mr. Ponn said. Aaden nodded. "But you see, there is much more to it. I expect you might have told one of your friends about it and he tried it and nothing happened. True?" Again Aaden nodded. "This is because most people have to go through training to even know how to say a spell. Because you have the *X* on your wrist from touching a dragon at birth, you have the power to do magic.

"Tomorrow morning at eight o'clock you will all go to Beginners' Magic. After that, you will go to the courtyard for Beginners' Sword Fighting, followed by Archery and Horseback Riding. Now, go to the second story and find Room 258. That's where you'll be staying. Oh, and Aaden, every day after classes you will be able to visit your dragon. Here are maps of the academy for all of you," Mr. Ponn said, handing them out to the boys.

Academy

Go to classes every day—
isn't that what you do
at an academy?
Perfect attendance,
Perfect grades,
That's what they tell me.
But couldn't there possibly
be something more to an
academy?

Chapter 5

"My name is Ms. Mote, and I will be your Beginners' Magic teacher. The first spell you will learn is very basic. It gives your target a cut about an inch long. I'd like you all to concentrate as hard as you can on my hand and say the words *krarder don.* Since you are all beginners, no harm shall come to me." She pointed to a small, red-haired boy in the front row. "You can start, and we will go row by row until everybody has had a chance," the teacher said, holding out her hand.

"*Krarder don!*" the boy yelled. Nothing happened. "*Krarder don!*" Nothing. "*Krarder don!*" Still nothing. And so it continued, with each student saying "*Krarder don!*" without result. And then it was Aaden's turn.

"*Krarder don!*" Splat! A cut half an inch long formed in the center of Ms. Mote's palm.

"Aahh!" she yelled, more out of surprise than pain. She hadn't expected a beginner to perform a spell on his first day.

"I am so sorry, Ms. Mote."

"No problem. I have bandages. Class, jog in place while I'm gone." The students looked puzzled but got up and ran in place nonetheless. Ms. Mote pulled out a bandage from her desk and started walking to the door. "You come with me, boy." Aaden followed her, feeling worried. Was he going to be expelled? Just then, the teacher opened a wooden door that led into a brick room identical to the one he had been in the day before. "Say the following spells after me. *Hoper kan.*"

"*Hoper kan!*" A rock flew and hit a brick and Aaden's X continued to shine.

"*Alpha kan.*"

"*Alpha kan!*" The rock disappeared.

"Follow me." Ms. Mote opened the door and walked down the hall and into another classroom, followed by Aaden, who was dying from anticipation.

"Mr. Tohe, this youngster is ready for your class," she said, addressing the teacher. Ms. Mote left to return to her classroom.

"What is your name?" Mr. Tohe asked.

"Aaden."

"Well, then, go over there by the window and make yourself comfortable." Aaden walked over to the window and sat down.

Mr. Tohe went to his desk and pulled out a textbook. He handed the book titled *Intermediate Magic* to Aaden. "Right now the students are just flipping through their books and practicing different spells on the wood. But do not practice any of the spells past page 300 unless you are in one of the ten brick rooms around the academy." Aaden nodded and started flipping through the book. At the beginning of the book, it said that the more one practiced a spell, the more effective it became. "Interesting," he said quietly to himself.

"Class, turn to page 132, please," Mr. Tohe said. The students flipped through the pages for a minute until they reached the correct page. "Look in the middle of the right page. One of the spells should form ice around an object. Starting with the new student, I want all of you to say the spell, one at a time."

"*Vater ron!*" Aaden yelled. The usual happened: first he felt his X hurt and shine red, then something happened to the place he was looking at. This time, a thin piece of ice about six inches long hit the middle of the wood and then disappeared in a few moments.

"*Vater ron!*" the student next to Aaden said. The same thing happened, except that boy didn't have an X. After that, the spells were quick and there were shorter intervals between spells, and soon everybody in the circle had tried the spell.

"Now, class, on the count of three, I want all of you to focus that spell right above the wood and then imagine bringing it down to the top of the wood," Mr. Tohe said. "*Vater ron!*" the class yelled together. Just then, something amazing happened. Instead of thirty pieces of ice hitting each other in midair, thirty beams of blue light collided above the wood and made one big ball of light. Then, as the students imagined moving the ball downward, it did. Just as the ball hit the wood, a crust of ice formed all over the wood.

"*Ervin wak!*" Mr. Tohe yelled, and a fiery heat melted the ice away.

"Why didn't it make a bunch of ice instead of that blue ball?" one of the students asked.

"A good question, Siumen. That is very tough to explain, even for scientists who study the subject. I'm oversimplifying, but when two or more spells are emitted, they each sense the other magic and combine into a single beam. Oh, look at the time! Off to your next lesson. Aaden, I'll show you the way to your next class."

Mr Tohe directed him to go down another hallway and through an archway into another large underground courtyard. It had an immense ceiling and was well lit, so there must have been numerous unseen vents overhead. He walked toward a group of students who were standing around a tall stocky middle-aged man.

"Hello, class," the teacher said. Looking at Aaden and his friends, who had been reunited for this class, he continued, "And for you new students, my name is Mr. Ratchet. To begin our day, I'd like everybody to jog in place for three minutes." The students began jogging in place. "Raise those knees higher, Hoder! That's it, that's it. And…slow down. Come over here and pick out swords and shields for yourselves," Mr. Ratchet said, nodding toward a giant pile of old and rusty shields and swords.

Everyone in the class except the Aader ran as fast as they could toward the pile and started ramming into each other in their haste to find the best equipment. "Huh," Faten sighed. By the time they got to the pile, the only sets left were all bent and covered with rust, and one shield even had a green stain on it.

"Just our luck," Drakint said, slowly picking up a set. The rest of the group followed, and they walked back to the circle.

"Everybody get with a partner and begin fighting. Careful, though, don't hurt your partner. Just stop the sword about three inches away," Mr. Ratchet said.

Cedar and Faten walked over to an empty area and started sparring. "I guess that leaves us, then," Drakint said. Drakint thrust his sword toward Aaden's stomach. Just in the nick of time, Aaden jerked his shield in front of his stomach, and the sword made a dent in his shield. This made them realize that they would never score points just throwing their swords forward; they would have to trick their opponents and throw a series of moves at them before the main attack.

Aaden pretended to strike near Drakint's left knee, and then pulled back his sword and pushed it near his opponent's right shoulder blade. Drakint dodged and aimed his sword at Aaden's heart. Aaden blocked Drakint's sword with his own. Every once in a while, Mr. Ratchet would go over to a pair and make suggestions.

By the end of class, everybody was panting and sweating. They were told to go to the other side of the underground courtyard for archery lessons.

When they got there, they noticed there were targets lined up against the stone walls. A few moments later, a walking suit of armor came clanking over to the class. "Hello, class. My name is Mr. Roke, and I, um, will be your...um, horseback—I mean archery, um, teacher," the man in the armor said slowly. The students who had been to this class before exchanged glances of curiosity. Mr. Roke continued, "As some of you know, I...um...am a new teacher. First, um, well…um, you know what to do." The students walked over to the pile of bows and arrows and each picked out one bow and seven arrows. Aaden wondered why they hadn't run.

Mr. Roke went over to the leftovers and chose a bow and arrows for himself. "Well, um, we're going to, um, aim for the closest target today. You know, for the, um…new students, if there, um, are any. So…um, just like, um…watch my, um…posture while I'm, you know, like, um, aiming. So, um, what you do is, um, you kind of just raise the, um…elbow in the back a little higher."

"Sir, we're supposed to keep our elbows even," a student said smugly, crossing his arms.

"Yeah, right, um, that's what I meant to say. So just watch me first." The teacher pulled back the string, and the arrow shot forward and hit the ground a few feet below the target. "Just, um, practice. Let me try, um, one more—"

"No, why don't you let me show you how it's done?" the smug student said.

"Ooooooh…" the class said in unison.

"Uh, yeah, why don't you, um, do that," said Mr. Roke.

The student walked to where the teacher was standing. He pulled back the string, closed one eye, and the arrow shot forward and hit the bull's-eye. "Woo hoo!" a few people cheered.

"What a show-off," Faten said.

"Typical," Cedar agreed.

The student walked back to rejoin his classmates, leaving Mr. Roke staring at the target. "Well, then, why don't you, um, go and, um, practice then?"

The class formed into groups and began shooting the arrows.

"I wonder why Mr. Ponn hired that man. He's worse than us," Faten said.

Brling! Cedar's arrow hit the right edge of the target. *Brling!* Aaden's arrow shot out and hit the row second to the bottom.

"Time for horseback riding!" Mr. Roke yelled, so he could be heard over the students' chatter. The class walked over to Mr. Roke and dropped their bows and arrows in a messy pile. Then most of the class started walking to another part of the courtyard, and the new students followed. They crossed the courtyard and found a robust-looking man surrounded by horses.

"Pick your usual horses and follow me, guys," the teacher said.

"Excuse me—we're new students and we don't know which horses to pick," Aaden said to the teacher.

"Oh, I see. Well, then, first off, I'm Mr. Speer. How old are you?" Mr. Speer asked.

"I'm sixteen," Aaden said.

"I'm fifteen," Cedar said.

"I'm fourteen," Drakint said. "And a half," he added quickly.

"I'm thirteen," Faten said.

"Well, then, for the eldest one we have the black horse over there. His name is Rac'quere." Aaden walked over to the horse and mounted. Lucky for the Aader, all of these horses were well-trained.

Mr. Speer said, "For the next oldest, we have the light brown one over there. His name is Browndere." Cedar walked over to the horse and mounted.

"For you," the man said, looking at Drakint, "we have the white horse back there called Silverhide." Drakint went over to his horse.

"And for you," Mr. Speer said, this time looking at Faten, "we have Alphid, the dark brown horse near the middle." Faten walked over to Alphid and mounted.

Mr. Speers addressed the entire class. "Everybody line up, with the new students in the back." The students obeyed. "Now, jump over the small bar and then go to the end of the line."

The teen in the front galloped forward on his white horse and leaped just in front of the iron bar. The next student did the same, and the next.

It was Cedar's turn. "Aah!" Cedar yelled as he and Browndere fell toward the ground.

"Stand back! I'll take care of this," Mr. Speer said. He walked over to Cedar (who was yelping in pain) and pulled a long piece of cloth from his pocket. "Are you bleeding anywhere?" the teacher asked. Cedar turned his arm over and revealed a huge scrape that was bleeding. Most of the students either closed their eyes or turned away. "Oh, dear. This cloth will have to do." Mr. Speer wrapped the cloth around the wound while Cedar yelled every few seconds. "Roedin, take this kid to the nurse. Be careful with him, though."

The student nodded and helped Cedar up. Then he took Cedar's good arm around his neck and together they walked toward a door that led out of the courtyard.

"No matter. Let's keep going, then. Who's next?" Mr. Speer asked hastily. Aaden raised a wobbly hand. Then, conjuring up all of his strength and shaking off the fear that he would fall down like Cedar, he galloped forward. For a second, there was a green blur. Then he saw a piece of metal right in front of him, and Rac'quere jumped. Aaden thought he was going to fall, but he stayed on Rac'quere. He had made it! He realized he'd had his eyes closed during the jump. He opened them and saw Mr. Speer smiling at him.

"Good work," said Mr. Speer.

Chapter 6

"I'm going to see Harlume, okay? I'll meet you back in our dormitory later," Aaden said.

"Sure," Faten said.

"See you," Cedar added.

"Bye," Aaden said and walked down the corridor. He looked at his map of the second floor, which was where he was. According to the map, he had to go down a stairway that was right in front of him. Aaden looked up and saw two stairwells. *How curious*, he thought. He decided to take the one on the right.

This staircase is awfully long, he thought. Aaden had been walking down the staircase for about five minutes, and still there was no sign of a new floor anywhere below. Then he felt stone beneath his feet. He looked up and saw a dark corridor lit by only one candle next to the right-hand wall. When he reached the end of the hall, he saw a wooden door and opened it. It led to a small room made of stone with one table in its center. On the table sat a huge book labeled *Forgotten Magic*. "I must have reached one of those secret rooms Mr. Ponn was talking about," Aaden said out loud.

Just as he was about to pick up the book, he felt a cold breeze blow through the room. He picked up the book and ran out of the room and up the stairs as fast as he could. When he was on the second floor again, he turned around. The staircase had vanished. Then he remembered Harlume and headed down the other staircase.

Luckily, this was a normal staircase, and it led to a gigantic, well-lit room with an extremely high ceiling. In the room several dragons flew around, occasionally landing on a tree or eating a bird. Immediately Aaden saw Harlume lying on the grass, apparently sleeping. Aaden approached and gently patted the dragon's head. Harlume opened one eye, then he opened the other eye and stood up. The dragon bent low to the ground. At first, Aaden was confused, but then he understood. He swung one leg over Harlume's massive body and pushed himself up with the other. Harlume beat his wings and glided up into the air. The wind made Aaden's eyes water.

Harlume plunged and landed on the grass. Aaden looked at his timepiece. It read 6:53. "I have to go, Harlume. See you tomorrow," Aaden said, waving and walking toward the door. Harlume waved his wing. Aaden headed for his dormitory to drop off his book.

~   ~   ~

"Did you have a good time, Aaden?" Cedar asked at the dinner table.

"Yep. We had a nice flight." Just then, a man in a white suit came to the table and put down a big plate of turkey. Aaden took his fork and knife and cut off a small piece. It was delicious, and he suddenly realized how hungry he was.

"Yum," Drakint said after trying some. A different man in a white suit came and put down a huge platter of mashed potatoes and a smaller plate with dry bread and cheese. Aaden ate some mashed potatoes and drank some water.

"This is the best food I have ever tasted," he said.

"Same here," Cedar said.

"You bet," Drakint chimed in. "You should try some bread, Aaden; it's really good." Aaden put some cheese on top of a warm roll and dipped it in the bowl of lemon juice that had been delivered earlier. Like everything else, it was scrumptious.

About half an hour later, Cedar said, "I think I'm going to go to our dorm."

"I'm going too. I'm really full," said Faten, who always felt more comfortable when the group stuck together.

"I guess I'll go too, then," Drakint said, biting off a piece of the bread he held.

"I'm going to go to one of the brick rooms to practice some magic, okay?" Aaden said.

"Okay, bye," the other three said in unison.

Before leaving his dormitory, Aaden picked up the magic book he had found earlier and the one he had used during class. Then he walked out the door and pulled out his map of the second floor. He looked at the key and saw that the brick rooms were marked with red dots. According to the map, if he went straight and then turned left, he would find one.

When he got to the spot where there should be a brick room, Aaden saw a door that had a picture of a brick carved into it. He opened the door and saw that his reading of the map had been correct.

For about an hour or so, he flipped through both of his books, practicing a lot of spells that he thought would be useful in battle. Then he flipped to the back of the special magic book. The last spell was cast using the words "*alper kori.*" Below the spell, Aaden read: *Think before you use this spell. Some have died trying. The choice is up to you.* Aaden decided to try the spell. "*Alper kori!*" Aaden's *X* glowed red. There was a swirling mist of blackness. A dark figure wearing a hooded black cloak emerged from the mist. At once Aaden knew it was a shade, one of the most powerful and evil sorcerers ever known.

"*Alpha kon!*" Aaden yelled, trying to get rid of it.

"*Purid rok!*" the shade yelled. A blue light emitted from Aaden. A green light emitted from the shade's palm. The two spells collided. Aaden saw his *X* glow green, and then there was nothing but blackness.

~   ~   ~

There was a girl bending over Aaden's bed in the nurse's office. She had black, flowing hair that was very long. Her eyes were dark brown. She looked like she might be Aaden's age, or maybe a little bit younger. She was the most beautiful girl Aaden had ever seen.

"Hello, youngster. What did you do today? Fall off a horse? Get shot with an arrow?" An old nurse asked, breaking his dream-like state of peace. Aaden felt confused. Who had the girl of his dream been? Was she real?

"Magic," he sputtered out between his thoughts.

"Really? Now, then, let's get you something warm to drink," the nurse said, exiting the room.

She returned and said, "Here we go. Some nice hot cocoa to ease your mind." The nurse handed Aaden a warm mug full of hot cocoa.

"What happened?" Aaden asked quietly.

"Well, I am not exactly sure. The Intermediate Magic teacher knocked on the door and nobody answered, so he opened the door and found you, or so I'm told. If you want the details, ask him when you recover," the nurse said.

"But…but I've already recovered. I didn't get hurt or anything, I don't think," Aaden said.

"Oh, now, don't be too sure just yet. You're going to see the doctor, and we'll see if any of your bones are broken or something. Oh, here he comes right now."

A man wearing a cross between a white suit and a white robe came walking in through the door. "Hello. I am Dr. Hade, and I'm just going to check for broken bones or any bleeding, things of that sort. Don't worry, nothing that I'm going to do will hurt." The doctor pulled off Aaden's blanket and looked at his clothes. "No bleeding—a good sign. Now, if you could stand up for a moment, that would be great. I'm going to use our new heat-wave sensor to check for any broken bones," Dr. Hade said. Aaden stood up. The nurse flipped a switch and there was darkness in the room. Then she flipped another switch and a red circle appeared on the ground next to Aaden. She moved a joystick and positioned the light so it shone on Aaden. The doctor looked at a screen. "Nothing broken. Even better news. You're all set, then. You can resume your activities."

~   ~   ~

"What happened when I got knocked out, Mr. Tohe?" Aaden asked the teacher.

"Well, you tried to do a spell from a secret book, and you summoned a shade. That book was hidden away for a good reason. You tried to get rid of the shade using a spell. The shade tried to kill you with its magic, and the two magic beams hit each other. Luckily for you, you have an *X,* which absorbed some of the shade's magic, so it just knocked you out. Then I came in and tried to get rid of the shade. Under different circumstances, I probably would have died, but since you were there, your *X* absorbed a lot of the shade's powers, and I got rid of it," Mr. Tohe explained.

"But sir, how come my *X* didn't absorb a lot of the power when everyone in Intermediate Magic used a spell?" Aaden asked.

"Because your *X* can tell when magic is coming from someone on your side or from someone opposing you. It knew that the class was on your side, so it didn't absorb the magic," Mr. Tohe answered. "Now go to your place by the window. I have a class to teach, and I also must make an important announcement."

"Okay," Aaden said, walking to the window.

"Now, class, before we start our magic class, I have an extremely important thing to say, so listen carefully. As most of you already know, there are many kingdoms who are after us. Word has reached us that a scout has found our hiding place, and there is going to be a war within a few days. One at a time, starting with Aaden, each of you will come over to me and I will set you up with armor, a sword, and a shield. While you are waiting for your turn, try to work together to do different spells. Come, then, Aaden, time is a-wasting," Mr. Tohe said. Aaden walked over to the teacher.

The armor was very heavy and painful. It was hard even to walk without hurting himself. But in a war, Aaden preferred to be in armor to being without it. Aaden thought the armor was kind of small for him, but he didn't want to try on another suit.

"Try this sword," Mr. Tohe said, handing one to Aaden. Aaden swung it around and stabbed the air with the metal blade.

"It's fine," he said.

"And what about this shield?" the teacher asked. He picked up a shield with a picture of a golden oak tree on it. Aaden picked it up. It was quite heavy. He didn't know if he would be able to defend himself with it during battle.

"It's kind of big," he said honestly.

"How about this one?" He gave Aaden a shield that looked exactly the same, only smaller. Aaden took it and swung it around.

"It's okay," he said.

"Well, then, now that we have that settled, you can go back to your dorm, take off all your armor, and put it somewhere safe. When you're done, come back to me," Mr. Tohe said. Aaden followed his teacher's directions and walked toward his room.

Aaden had a hard time taking off the armor. In the process, he got a few scratches. When he was finished, he looked at his time-piece. It read 9:36. The other students were probably on their way to Sword Fighting. He wondered why Mr. Tohe wanted to meet him.

By the time he got to the classroom, it was 9:43. "Hello, Aaden," Mr. Tohe said. "I am going train you separately from the class today. The reason is that I see great potential in you. Now, then, let's try some combat, okay? I trust that you've studied your magic book some?" Mr. Tohe said.

"Only a little," Aaden said, finding it easy to be honest with Mr. Tohe.

"*Vater wret!*" the teacher yelled. Unlike when Aaden said the magic words, a huge piece of ice about two feet long and one foot in diameter flew toward Aaden. Aaden thought for a moment and then remembered something from the beginning of one of his books. "*Vater wret dullur!*" Aaden yelled. A green beam of light surrounded the ice, and then both disappeared. "*Rogerin racqued!*" Mr. Tohe yelled. The piece of wood in the center of the classroom rose up from the floor and sped toward Aaden. "*Rogerin racqued pudder!*" Aaden yelled. Aaden felt himself losing power. He concentrated as hard as he could. All of a sudden, the pressure was gone and the piece of wood went back to its place. Mr. Tohe looked surprised.

"*Alama kalaza!*" Aaden yelled. A sword made of mist moved toward Mr. Tohe. Mr. Tohe was very surprised. A look of fear came over his face, and he didn't move. "*Alama kalaza duller!*" Aaden yelled. Another green light swallowed the sword and they both disappeared.

"What happened?" Aaden asked. "Why didn't you get rid of it?"

Mr. Tohe ran out of the room as fast as he could. "What the...?" Aaden said. Why had his teacher run away from him?

Aaden heard the door open. In came Mr. Ponn, followed by Mr. Tohe. Aaden did not move a muscle. His mind was full of questions, but he did not say a word.

"Aaden, do you know what you just did?" Mr. Ponn asked. Aaden shook his head. "You just performed one of the most ancient spells known—a spell that even I cannot do. In fact, there is only one person who was known to have the ability to use that spell. Now you understand why your teacher was a little bit frightened. But don't worry: this is not bad news. Actually, it is good news. I think it's time for you to have some special training with me. I know you will be a big help during the war. Come, then, to my office," Mr. Ponn said.

Aaden was speechless on the way to Mr. Ponn's office. Why was he so special? Why couldn't his friends be like him too?

"Aaden, I am going to teach you a spell that few people know. It has long been a family secret. I think you can master it. The spell has the ability to knock out or even kill many people at the same time, if used correctly. The catch is that when you use it, you take the risk of killing yourself. Many people have tried unsuccessfully and been killed by the spell. Even if you master the spell, you can use it only a few times in your life. Today I am asking you if you would like me to train you to be able to use this spell. Just be sure you've thought hard before you make your decision, though," Mr. Ponn said.

Aaden thought hard for a few minutes. He needed to be able to protect the school and his friends. He needed to find a way to return to his injured friend Rederin and save him. He really didn't see how he could refuse the chance to learn as much as he could. "I will try the training, sir," he said.

Over the next few days, Aaden spent nearly all his time doing numerous exercises with Mr. Ponn. One cold morning, while he was training with Mr. Ponn, a loud alarm sounded. "Aaden, go to your dorm room and put on your suit of armor. Come back here with your shield. There will be no need for your sword. And hurry!" Mr. Ponn said.

Aaden ran out the door. The corridors were filled with frantic students. Everyone was running to the dormitories. Aaden spotted his friends and ran after them.

"Do you know what's happening, guys?" he asked them, panting.

"No, just that we're supposed to meet in the courtyard," Faten said, also panting.

"The courtyard? Mr. Ponn told me to meet him in his office," Aaden said.

Drakint opened the door to their dormitory and said, "We'll talk later. Right now, we've got to hurry!"

Aaden ran over to his suit of armor and put it on as fast as he could, trying not to grimace from discomfort. When he finished, he ran out the door and went to Mr. Ponn's office.

"Aaden. Follow me; it's time for war," Mr. Ponn said. Mr. Ponn was wearing a full suit of armor himself, and like Aaden, he had a shield but no sword. Mr. Ponn led Aaden up a flight of stairs, which went to a large patio area overlooking a wide valley. From there Aaden could see an army on horses riding closer. The only people on the patio were Mr. Ponn, Aaden, and Mr. Tohe. "Aaden, we three are the best at doing magic. That is why we will be up here shooting magic down at the enemy while the rest of the academy and staff will be down there on horses, fighting with some magic, but mostly with their swords. Now, get ready. *Fire!*" Mr. Ponn yelled.

The army was now very close. The soldiers saw the patio (but not the three on it), and started pounding their fists and piercing the mountainside below it. Mr. Ponn and Mr. Tohe started muttering spells so fast that Aaden couldn't even tell what they were saying. But as the words came out of their mouths, fiery blasts sprung from their fingertips, shooting down into the army below. The soldiers who were hit by these blasts were knocked off their horses and onto the ground. They didn't get up again. Ice and fire went pouring down. Some of the knights and horses flew up into the air and then smashed back down to the ground, killing others.

"Aaden, do the sword spell! *Now!*" Mr. Ponn yelled to Aaden in between his spells.

"*Alama kalaza!*" Aaden yelled with all his might. A huge sword made of mist shot straight toward the army. By this time, the enemies had noticed the spells, and they tried to stop them, but the three on the patio were too strong for them. Then they saw the magic sword and started running frantically to escape it. Many of them were killed by it, but then a lot of them put a spell together and forced the sword to disappear.

"*Alama kalaza!*" Aaden yelled again, but this time nothing happened. Then the army finally broke in. Everywhere there were the loud sounds of metal clashing and people screaming. The young dragonriders tried to force the army back outside, so the three on the patio could keep attacking. Their foes were numerous, and their situation looked bleak.

But then, almost out of nowhere, ten or so dragons arrived on the scene and began shooting flames at the army. Pretty soon the entire battlefield was covered with smoke. When the smoke subsided, only the dragonriders were there. Oddly enough, there weren't many bodies visible in the debris.

"Everybody, this war is over! Go back to your activities!" Mr. Ponn yelled, but there was no panic or fear in his voice. If Aaden hadn't known better, he might have thought Mr. Ponn was calling the students back inside after a fire drill. Aaden wondered how often these wars occurred. The dragonriders walked back into the building.

"Good job, Aaden. The sword spell worked very well," Mr. Tohe said.

"Thanks," Aaden replied.

"Well, then, Aaden, let's continue our training," Mr. Ponn said, walking down the stairs.

As the days progressed, Aaden began to feel more confident about his magical ability. But he missed seeing his friends during classes. "Aaden, do you feel like you've had enough lessons?" Mr. Ponn asked.

"I'm not sure," Aaden replied.

"Well, I feel like you've learned enough for now. I have a special quest for you. Would you fly to your former home, the kingdom of Dragondaire, and steal the kingdom's Ruishi Crystal? Now, before you give your answer, I want you to know that we don't just want to steal from the kingdom. We need the crystal in order to keep our hideout safe. You see, the crystal has magical properties that can serve the Dragonriders' Academy of Learning and Secrets very well," Mr. Ponn said.

"Sir, I grew up in Dragondaire. Don't you think it might be betraying them if I stole from them?" Aaden asked.

"Aaden, I know you're from Dragondaire—that's one of the reasons I chose you. They won't see you as an enemy. That will make it easier to get the crystal," Mr. Ponn explained. "Why don't you think it over tonight?"

"Okay. Bye, Mr. Ponn," Aaden said, walking out of the room.

When Aaden got to his dorm, he lay on his bed. Did he really want to do this? Would his father be disappointed in him if he were to found out? Would he even succeed in retrieving the Ruishi Crystal? But wouldn't a true dragonrider accept a challenge like this? In the end, Aaden decided to take on the quest. He imagined bringing back the crystal and everyone being proud of him.

Aaden got up very early that morning. He walked to Mr. Ponn's office. "Mr. Ponn, I have decided to go on the quest," he said.

"That's great. And trust me, if you succeed, it will be worth it. Why don't you get your dragon and meet me in the courtyard," Mr. Ponn said, looking especially cheerful.

Aaden hurried outside and went down the staircase that led to the place where the dragons stayed. "Come on, Harlume! We're going to go on a quest!" Aaden yelled to his dragon. Saying the words made him feel even more excited. Harlume flew toward Aaden, then they both walked up a large ramp for dragons next to the stairwell leading to the second floor.

"We're going to go back to Dragondaire and get the Ruishi Crystal to help this academy. I'm so excited!" Aaden said to Harlume.

At the courtyard, Mr. Ponn asked, "Are you ready?"

"I've never been more ready," Aaden replied, mounting his dragon.

"Good luck!" Mr. Ponn yelled.

"I'll be back!" Aaden yelled back from the air.

"Bye!" Mr. Ponn yelled to the green dot in the sky.

To Aaden, flying was the most fun thing there could ever be. The wind brushing by his face as he was level with the clouds was simply wonderful.

But after about an hour, Aaden began to get cold, and the wind started making his eyes blink incessantly. Before, hours had felt like minutes, but now minutes felt like hours. Then Aaden looked down and saw the familiar kingdom of Dragondaire. "Here we are, Har- lume. Let's land." Harlume began a dive toward the trees. Aaden braced him against the intense discomfort of losing altitude so fast. Finally they landed on soft moss, in sight of the castle.

Chapter 7

"Hello, I'm looking for the Ruishi Crystal. Could you point me in the right direction?" Aaden said to the guards in front of the castle door.

"Oh, yes. If you follow the stairwell up to the tallest room and go in the door, you will find it," the guard said in a deep voice.

"Could my dragon come up with me?" Aaden asked.

"As long as he doesn't break anything," the guard replied.

"Thank you for your help," Aaden said. He went into the castle and started up the stairs. As he walked, Harlume flapped his wings in place to make himself go higher.

At the top of the stairs, Aaden opened the door. "Just wait here for me," he whispered to Harlume. "And be ready to fly." Aaden walked into the room. It was empty except for a small wooden stool in the center. On the stool there was an empty, broken glass box. *What the...? Somebody must have gotten here first,* Aaden said to himself. He ran out the door.

"It's been taken. Let's warn the guard," Aaden ran down the stairs and to the door. When Harlume landed, they both went outside.

"The Ruishi Crystal is gone, sir. I just went up to see it, and the box was broken," Aaden said.

"Really?" the guard asked suspiciously. "Thanks for telling me. I'll go and tell the king." The guard ran into the castle. Just then, Aaden saw three boys in black sneaking toward a dragon.

"They have the crystal," he whispered to Harlume. "Let's go." He jumped onto Harlume's back and pointed at the boys. "Hurry! They're getting away on that dragon!" Harlume pumped his wings, rose into the air, and started flying toward the other dragon. When they got closer, Aaden noticed some details about the other dragon. It was dark blue and much thinner than any other dragon he had seen. It also had huge wings.

The dragon beat its wings backwards once, and then off it shot like an arrow. "Wow!" Aaden exclaimed. "That dragon's fast." Harlume did the same and put on a burst of speed, but was no match for the dragon up ahead.

"Hey, look, I think they're stopping to sleep. That will be the perfect time to attack," Aaden said hopefully. Sure enough, the band was stopping to rest in a clearing. As quietly as possible, Harlume landed near where the boys were sleeping. As quiet as a mouse, he sprinted over to them. When he reached the clearing, one of the boys jumped up. "Wake up, guys. We've got someone to take care of," the boy said. The other boys jumped up too. Up close, they looked like triplets.

The three boys slowly raised their hands. "*Rogerin racqued!*" they yelled in unison. Three green lights combined into one big ball. The ball hit a large boulder, then the boulder sped toward Aaden. Aaden's *X* glowed green and the rock slowed down. "*Vater wret!*" Aaden yelled. Three pieces of ice smacked the boys' faces. Again, the boys slowly moved their hands up. Then the three yelled, "*Ervin wak!*" A large ball of fire sped toward Aaden. Aaden's *X* turned green and the ball of fire began to grow smaller and slower until the wind blew it out. The three boys looked puzzled. Obviously, they hadn't heard about *X* marks.

"*Alama kalaza!*" Aaden yelled. The familiar sword of mist appeared and stabbed two of the boys in the chest, knocking them out. The third boy picked up the Ruishi Crystal, jumped onto his dragon, and flew away. Luckily, the sword of mist could reach speeds of up to three hundred miles per hour, and it sped toward the dragon. Aaden jumped onto Harlume, and they flew toward the sword.

Aaden saw the blue dragon plummet to the ground. When he got there, Aaden saw the boy lying next to the dragon. He walked over to him and pulled the crystal from his hand.

"Aah!" Aaden yelled as an arm came out of nowhere and pressed into Aaden's throat. He caught a glimpse of Harlume flying above, but then a man slapped his left cheek and all he saw was blackness.

Hours later, he found himself in a jail cell, behind iron bars. This time four guards holding axes and swords were facing him.

He felt weak, like he had not eaten in days. But he stood up. Just then, a tray was passed under a flap. On it he saw one piece of bread and one bowl of water. Aaden took a bite of the bread. It was hard and tasted stale, but at least Aaden didn't pass out like he had before. Immediately, he gained energy and decided to try a spell on the guards.

"*Alama kalaza!*" Aaden yelled. His *X* shone red. Another sword of mist came out of nowhere and started stabbing the guards. The guard closest to Aaden shoved a sword at him through a space between two bars, but Aaden dodged just in time. He saw that the sword had knocked out all of the guards. Then the sword disappeared. "*Rogerin racqued!*" Aaden yelled. The bars moved out of their places and then fell to the ground. Aaden walked out of the cell. He looked at one of the guards and saw the Ruishi Crystal clutched in his hand. Aaden picked it up and went to search for Harlume.

Finally he glimpsed his dragon in a cell surrounded by ten guards carrying sticks, axes, and swords. Aaden jumped out, facing the guards, who came charging at him. "*Ervin wak!*" Aaden yelled. Eight balls of fire knocked down the guards and broke the iron bars. They were just about to hit Harlume when Aaden yelled, "*Ervin wak duller!*" A green light swallowed the balls of flame and they disappeared. He yelled, "Come on, Harlume! Let's go!"

Harlume flew over to Aaden. Just then, Aaden heard footsteps. He jumped onto Harlume and they flew out the door and into the open sky.

"Let's go back to the Frosty Mountains. I have the crystal," Aaden said to Harlume, and they began their perilous journey back.

The two were about halfway to the Frosty Mountains when Aaden heard a distant beating of wings. Aaden turned his head and saw a band of red dragons. At first, Aaden thought they were more dragonriders, but they had no riders. "Oh, no. Wild dragons! There are wild dragons behind us, Harlume!" Harlume turned his head and saw the dragons. The red dragons gained speed and were soon level with Harlume on his right side. Harlume was forced to go left, which was the wrong way. The red dragons caught up with them on the right again, and again Harlume was forced to turn left. The same thing happened again, and Harlume again turned left and then left again, until they were going in the right direction. But this time, the red dragons came from behind and started shooting flames at Harlume and Aaden.

"You keep us going in the right direction, Harlume. I'll take care of them," Aaden said to Harlume. "*Alama kalaza!*" Aaden yelled. The sword of mist went speeding toward the dragons, stabbing each of them in turn. But since the dragons were so strong, the sword only made them drop a little bit lower and slowed them down for a few moments.

Luckily, the sword did not disappear; it just kept on stabbing. Aaden looked down and saw little figures that looked like the dragonriders fighting a huge army. *Those are not just wild dragons! They're* evil *dragons!* "Come on! Dive for your life, Harlume!" Aaden yelled. Harlume plunged quickly and hurtled toward the battleground. Just then, Aaden saw thousands of snakes fall from above. These snakes had four legs with sharp black talons. Aaden looked up and saw the red dragons pulling themselves upright from their upside-down position and flying away.

Ping! The snakes' talons pierced the ice of the battlefield. The snakes disappeared into the mountain. "Keep flying above the field, Harlume. I will shoot spells at them as we fly," Aaden said. "*Alama Kalaza!*" The sword of mist went toward the enemies and started stabbing them. "*Vater wret!*" A hundred or so small pieces of ice hit the helmets of the soldiers. Aaden watched as his sword disappeared. Just then he saw Mr. Ponn starting to cast a spell from the balcony. "*Rogerin racqued!*" Aaden yelled at the same time. The two green beams of light combined and moved toward a large oak tree. Using all his strength, Aaden helped pull it out of the ground. Then they both sent it straight to part of the army.

"Aah!" Mr. Ponn yelled. Aaden saw a few of the snakes appear out of the ground and try to bite Mr. Ponn.

"To the balcony!" Aaden yelled to Harlume. "You go and start attacking without me. I'll help Mr. Ponn."

Aaden jumped off his dragon onto the balcony. "*Ervin wak!*" he yelled. Three balls of flame killed the snakes and then disappeared.

"Aaden, did you get the crystal?" Mr. Ponn was weak, but business came first. Aaden reached into his pocket and pulled out the rock. Mr. Ponn said, "Follow me. Quickly!"

Mr. Ponn led Aaden down the long staircase and then up another staircase into a place that reminded Aaden of a bell tower without a bell. There were openings on each of the five sides of the small pentagonal room. In the middle, there was a tall altar covered with a small velvet blanket.

"Can I see the crystal?" Mr. Ponn asked. Aaden took it out of his pocket and gave it to Mr. Ponn. Mr. Ponn slowly placed it on the altar. "Aaden, stand directly in front of it with your arms spread apart."

Aaden did as he was told. All of a sudden, he saw a blinding ray of blue light come out of the crystal and hit him on the chest. For one moment, Aaden had an extraordinary feeling that he could not possibly put into words, and then it went away. At that moment,

Aaden felt a sense of safety deep inside him. He felt stronger and more confident about himself.

Just then, Aaden felt fire hit the right side of his stomach. "*Ervin duller!*" Mr. Ponn yelled. The fire disappeared, but Aaden's side was still stinging unmercifully. Mr. Ponn rushed over to him and helped him down the stairs and to the nurse's office.

A girl with long black hair walked into the room where Aaden was lying on a bed. Aaden recognized her as the girl from the dream he'd had when he was last in the nurse's office.

"This might hurt a little, but it will feel better in a little while," the girl said quietly. She walked over to a counter and picked up a small bottle. Then she walked over to Aaden again and squirted the liquid onto the place where the fire had hit. It was very painful, but Aaden did not scream, because he didn't want the girl to think he was weak.

Good Deeds

Do something wrong;
Misbehave,
Just come to me—
I am the man of
Good deeds,
I will guide you through life,
Assigning you a good deed if
Necessary
So if you do something wrong,
Just come to me,
And everything
Will be all right.

Chapter 8

Aaden watched as bunches of people came into the nurse's office. It had been a bloody war. Many people had been killed.

"Come, Aaden. I'd like to talk to you in private," Mr. Ponn said. Aaden was led down a staircase and into Mr. Ponn's office. "Please seat yourself," Mr. Ponn said as he sat down. Aaden took a seat in front of Mr. Ponn. "Aaden, you have heard that we lost the war, correct?" Mr. Ponn asked. Aaden shook his head, surprised by the news.

"Well, then, I guess I'll summarize what happened for you," Mr. Ponn said. "I came back to the balcony after I took you to the nurse, and I saw thousands of those little snakes appearing out of nowhere on the battlefield, killing the dragonriders. It was then that I realized that to save the lives of the remaining dragonriders, I must surrender. 'Peace!' I yelled over the roaring battle cries of the enemy. Everyone stopped their fighting and stared up at me.

"When the enemy realized what I meant, they summoned their snakes and yelled back to me. They said to give them gold and jewels, or else they would not accept our surrender! Though it pained me to do so, I told my elf helpers to give them some of our riches. When the enemy got them, they laughed and rode away on their horses. But I think I know how to defeat them the next time they come.

"On the entire surface of Peydran, there are seven legendary crystals, one of which is the Ruishi Crystal. Legend has it that whoever accumulates all of the crystals will have legendary powers. I am hoping that you will be that person—the person who will save us in the next war. I want you to think it over carefully, for it will be a very difficult job," Mr. Ponn finished. Mr. Ponn knew he needed Aaden's help, but he was genuinely concerned for his safety and knew that Aaden was exhausted from the day's events.

That night, Aaden had a hard time sleeping. When he finally did go to sleep, he had the weirdest dream. First he saw himself and the Aader in the suits they had used as disguises when stealing the horses. They stole the horses and rode away into the woods, just like it happened before. Then he saw the war that had happened only a few hours ago, in precise detail, as his classmates and friends perished in the battle with the flying snakes. After that he slept very soundly. He was happy to see his friends in the morning.

"Last night I had the weirdest dream. I saw us stealing the horses, and then I saw the war," Aaden said to the Aader during breakfast.

"That's the exact same dream I had!" Faten said.

"Me too," Cedar said.

"Well, I had a dream about becoming the king of Dragondaire," Drakint said. The rest of the Aader stared at Drakint before moving on.

"Weird. Very weird," Cedar said.

"Do you think it means that the war was lost because of us?" Aaden asked.

"Either that or it was an amazing coincidence," Faten said.

"I think we should probably talk to Mr. Ponn about it," Cedar said.

"Me too," Aaden said.

"I think it's better than just sitting here," Faten said.

"Okay, fine. We can go and just let Mr. Ponn solve this *issue* that's so important to you," Drakint said. He had never been very good at being sarcastic.

The boys went off to seek Mr. Ponn and were granted an audience with him in a surprisingly short time.

"Mr. Ponn, we wanted to ask you something. You see, we all—I mean, all of us except Drakint—had the same dream that showed us stealing horses and then it showed the war. Do you think it was a coincidence, or were we meant to have the dreams?" Aaden said.

"I, in fact, had a...similar dream. I do not think it was a coincidence. Bad deeds often yield bad effects. I'm not sure if I'm right, but I think all of you will have to do good deeds to make up for your bad ones. You see, I have never met a dragonrider who did bad things, and we have never lost a war. Do you want to just wait and see if we'll win the next war and things get better, or do you want to do good deeds to make up for your bad ones?" Mr. Ponn replied.

"I think we should do the good deeds," Aaden said.

"Well, I've heard news from my carrier pigeons that there was a giant smire on the island of Alpha Capa. It might be hard to help the villagers, but you might want to go there so you can do a good deed," Mr. Ponn said.

The group shuddered. Although none of them had ever experienced a smire firsthand, they were well aware of the giant storm's horrific powers. Everyone stared at Aaden.

"I'll do it," he said, by now accustomed to taking on seemingly impossible tasks.

Mr. Ponn showed no sign of surprise. He said that the rest of them could take on other tasks while Aaden was gone. After some discussion, they began preparations to leave the next day.

The next morning, Mr. Ponn led the Aader to the back of the academy on the same floor as the entrance, and to a door labeled, DRAGONROOM. He opened the door and revealed a gargantuan space. In was so large that the ceiling maintained twenty feet above magnificent oaks that towered ten yards high. There were deer, large birds and even a lake. But, the most extraordinary things were the dragons. Some were lying down, gazing dreamily into the lake, others were perching high on the oaks, and some were gliding in circles. Surprisingly, none seemed to be eating.

"Aaden, you can get your dragon. And the rest of you can choose dragons, or let the dragons choose you," Mr. Ponn said.

Aaden found Harlume and called out to him. When Harlume flew down, Aaden quickly explained the situation to him.

"Here's a map for you, Aaden. Alpha Capa is the small island right there on the Omega Sea," Mr. Ponn said, handing Aaden a piece of parchment. "Be very careful, and just to warn you, it might be a little harder than you think."

"Okay. Bye, Dragonmaster Ponn! Bye Faten, Cedar, and Drakint!" Aaden yelled as Harlume soared up by the balcony stairs.

"Raaaaahhhhhhrrrr!" Harlume yelled, only moments into flight. Aaden saw a wooden arrow protruding from Harlume's left wing. He looked down and saw a fleet of pirate ships shooting arrows at him. After a few more deep wounds, Harlume could not manage to keep flying, and he plummeted to the sea. Aaden screamed. But instead of feeling water, Aaden felt hot sand when he fell.

"We've made it to a..." Aaden began as he looked around. "Deserted island," he finished. He walked over to Harlume's wings and carefully pulled out the arrows. Just then a yellow squirrel-like creature came out of a bush and swiped its bushy tail over Harlume's wounds. Amazingly, the wounds and blood disappeared. Aaden stared in amazement. He had only ever read about squice in books. "Thank you, Mr. Squice," Aaden said to the animal. The squice nodded its head, bowed, and disappeared.

Aaden pulled out his map and opened it. He looked for the place on the map where the island should be, but found nothing. This was very odd, but realizing how hungry he was, he decided to rest and eat the lunch he had brought from the school.

"Let's fly further inland and look for berries," he said to his dragon, glad he had a friend to talk to.

After a little while, Aaden looked down and saw a fairly large clearing with red berries on most of the bushes around the perimeter. "Downward!" he yelled over the roaring winds, and down they plunged. After Aaden dismounted, Harlume flew away. At first

Aaden was confused, but then he realized that Harlume was probably hunting for meat and would be back shortly.

As he was picking and eating berries, Aaden thought he heard something. He looked up and saw a soldier of some sort riding toward the clearing. Aaden dove under the bushes. He heard the soldier walking around the clearing and then leaving. After a couple of minutes, he heard more footsteps, and then Harlume landed next to him. Apparently, the dragon had seen soldiers approaching and come to take Aaden out of harm's way. Aaden jumped onto Harlume. One, two, three beats and Harlume was in the air, leaving the small group of knights staring toward the sun.

"We need to go east," Aaden said. They went east.

"I think I see the island. Right down there," Aaden said only minutes later. According to the map, he was correct. Harlume was getting faster these days.

When they landed, Aaden was horrified to see thousands of houses in ruins, and what looked like bodies lying on the sandy beach. But as he looked around, Aaden saw villages up ahead that looked unharmed. "Let's go over there, Harlume, I think we came here to help *them*," he said, pointing to the village. In agreement, Harlume nodded his head and bent down.

They arrived at the village. "Who are you?" a woman from the village asked suspiciously. She was wearing a light blue poncho, a leather skirt, and straw sandals.

"My name is Aaden and I am here to help with the relief effort," Aaden said, unoffended by the woman's tone. "And who are you?"

"My name is Shonaia. The villagers will be very happy to know we have support from other places. Why don't you follow me? I'll show you around," the woman said more warmly. Aaden agreed and followed Shonaia.

"This is our water storage area. Because of the smire, our supply is very low," Shonaia said. In front of Aaden were no more than ten large barrels, each filled halfway to the top. "There are more of these in the village, but a lot of the water is contaminated. The problem is that we are not sure which barrels are safe. We only have one other system with fresh water, but that one is reserved for the wealthier villagers. Another problem is that the smire smashed many of our trees, damaging homes and other buildings, forcing many people to live outdoors. Because there is little fresh water, the live-stock have run off, and our fields are mostly in ruins, resulting in near starvation for our village. We fear deeply for our beloved children," Shonaia finished with a sigh. She showed him to a place where he could stay the night, and thanked him for coming, though she seemed to doubt his ability to help.

During the night, Aaden thought hard about what he could do for this village. He figured that the first thing would be to use his spells to make water. After that, he could help bring the farm animals back to the village. The villagers were weak and might not be able to do much.

It was sunrise when Aaden woke up with a sore back. To his surprise, when he went outside into the cold, he saw that many people were already outdoors. He walked over to a barrel and looked inside. It was nearly empty. Using all his strength, Aaden picked it up and emptied it.

"What are you doing, you foolish boy? Do not just dump out our scarce water supply!" a villager yelled.

"I will fill this barrel with fresh water," Aaden said simply. "*Arogan!*" Aaden yelled. A little bit of water went into the barrel. "*Arogan!*" More water went into the barrel. As Aaden continued creating water, it came in larger quantities. A crowd gathered to watch the amazing boy create water. Seeing his sweaty reflection in the barrel, Aaden saw that the barrel was full. "Dig in," he said quietly, but the whole village heard and rejoiced.

Casting spells was exhausting. Aaden decided to take a rest before attempting any more spells, so he went back into his small room and went to sleep.

When he woke up in the early afternoon, he felt even weaker than he had been a few hours earlier. But knowing what he had to do, he went back outside and saw that the barrel he had filled only a few hours ago had barely any water left.

"Hey, look! It's the water kid!" a child yelled when he saw Aaden. The villagers looked up and ran towards Aaden.

"Come on, then! Make us more water!" a villager yelled.

"*Arogan!*" Aaden yelled. Some water poured into the barrel. "*Arogan!*" A little bit more water flowed into the barrel. Aaden continued in this way for about half an hour until he needed another rest and went back to sleep.

Meanwhile, Cedar and Faten were on the island of Rapid Falls, learning how to shoot arrows at the wildlife.

"Hold your left elbow a little bit higher...perfect!" their instructor said enthusiastically. "Have you ever practiced shooting arrows before?"

"A little bit. We both did," Cedar replied.

"Because I think you're ready to hunt some game. Are you up for it?" the teacher said.

"That's what we came here for," Faten said.

The instructor left the boys at the edge of the woods. As they were walking in the woods, Cedar thought he heard rustling in the bushes. "I've got this one," he said, more to himself than to his brother. He pulled out an arrow from his quiver and placed it to his bow, stretching the string. All of a sudden a snake shot out from a bush and headed toward Faten. *Brling!* Cedar shot the arrow at the snake in a heartbeat.

"That was scary," Faten said. Cedar walked over to the snake and put it in his bag.

"Come on, let's keep going. We have hungry villagers to feed," Cedar said. They continued walking deeper and deeper into the wood.

"Do you hear that?" Faten asked.

"Yeah. I think it might be a deer," Cedar replied. Excited, Faten pulled out an arrow and placed it on his bow. He pulled back the string and waited. All of a sudden, a brown animal darted away in the distance. *Brling!* Faten let go of the string and watched as the arrow soared toward the deer. It missed the animal by an inch.

"Oh, man. It was so close!" Faten said. Suddenly they heard a loud roar.

"It's a—a *lion!*" Cedar yelled frantically.

"*Run!*" Faten yelled.

The two boys ran as fast as they could until they were out of breath. "Do you think it's gone?" Faten asked.

"I don't know. But don't you think we should be at the village by now?" Cedar said. But both boys could see that the village was nowhere in sight.

"RAAAARRRRHHH!" The animal sounded closer than it had before.

"*Run!*" Cedar yelled this time. Once more the two brothers ran deeper and deeper into the woods, though they thought they were getting closer and closer to the peaceful village. Faten stopped dead in his tracks. In front of them was a purplish black castle.

Cedar turned around and saw a tan-colored shape leaping toward them from a distance. "I'd rather go there than be eaten by a lion!" Cedar said, running toward the gates of the castle.

"Lion! Coming! We need to get in!" Cedar panted to the guard. The guard looked behind Cedar and saw the lion. He smiled and calmly pulled a lever, as if the lion were a bunny. Behind the gates there was a giant courtyard filled with gravestones. The grass was brown and looked as if it hadn't been watered in years. The guard hit a red button on the gate and a loud alarm sounded. All of a sudden, the massive doors leading to the castle were hauled open by two dwarves who looked like slaves. Then a giant figure came through the doors and walked onto the courtyard grass. It was a dark purple dragon.

But the dragon was not the thing that first caught the two boys' eyes. Rather, it was the woman riding on the dragon. She wore a long purple robe trimmed with white fur. She had pitch-black hair that ran down her back all the way to her waist. On her head sat a golden crown studded with gems.

Surrounding the dragon were four animals that looked like chee-tahs but had the heads of lions and green wings that looked much too large for the animals.

The woman called out to the boys. "Ah! You have come at last. I have waited a long time for you to come!" she said, producing a malevolent laugh that seemed to echo throughout the courtyard. "Come, then, boys! Follow me into the castle!" Cedar and Faten slowly walked up to the woman, almost entranced by the sight of her. She dismounted and walked across the courtyard and through a doorway, gesturing for the boys to follow her.

The room inside was cold and dark, lit only by a flickering candle. It was a small stone room, with a small table and chairs.

"Hurry up! Sit down! The *queen* does not have time for this. I have other things to do! But this is the most important thing right now," she said, sighing.

Cedar and Faten trembled as they sat in the hard chairs. The queen said, "Who sent you to look in the woods, my dear boys?" The two boys looked at each other, reading one another's thoughts. Both were equally afraid, and they did not say a word.

"Speak. I *will* get angry if you don't speak." Still, neither Faten nor Cedar spoke a word.

"Speak! You will go to prison, you *foolish* boys!" the queen said. The door was thrust open, and four guards grabbed the boys and carried them outside.

Once they were all out of earshot of the queen, one of the guards said, "Listen to me, boys. This queen is not a person you want to mess with! You understand? You'd better get out of here quick, or else!"

"We were forced to work here. Either that or die, or...or worse! Most of the people here are good people; they were just forced to do work for the queen," another guard whispered.

"One of the bad ones is the man who guards the gates. Not a drop of decent blood in his horrid body! We'll try to help you and visit you while you're in jail, but you're going to need to get out of here before the torture begins," the first guard said.

"Have a good time in jail. See you later," one of the guards said as they left Cedar and Faten behind bars. The boys understood that the guards were afraid to help them because the queen would punish them if she found out, so they tried to figure out what to do.

"How are we supposed to get of here?" Faten asked.

"Not a clue," Cedar replied, sighing. "Maybe someone will come to save us."

"What do you think the guards meant when they said 'or else'?" Faten asked.

"Something far worse than this," Cedar replied, trying not to sound as frightened as he was feeling.

Cedar and Faten heard footsteps coming down the hall. "I hope it's not that evil queen," Faten whispered. *Pit pat, pit pat, pit pat.* The person was coming nearer. All of a sudden, a man came through a corner door the boys hadn't noticed before. He had brown hair and seemed to be about fifty years old. He was wearing normal clothes, except for the humble crown of tarnished silver on his head. "We have to whisper. The queen can't find out that I'm here," the man said quietly.

"Are you the king?" Faten blurted out. He didn't mean to be rude, but it was the first thing on his mind.

"I am no king. She is no queen. She is a *sorcess.* She thinks she looks more like a real queen if she has me here as a 'king.' I am her personal slave, though. My life is of no importance. The only useful thing I've ever done was to help save one or two prisoners," the man said.

"What is a sorcess?" Cedar asked.

"Well, there are two armies of sorceresses on Rodan that are both pure evil. The queen of each army is called a sorcess. They are chosen by a process that nobody knows. Sorcesses are extremely strong and very rich. They like to have power. Wait! I think I hear someone coming. Got to go!" The man quickly ran to the door he had come in, opened it with a key, and dashed out.

The familiar *pit pat, pit pat* echoed through the hall as another visitor walked toward the two boys. And then—*whoosh!* The sorcess's robe swept around the corner. "Now, boys...are you ready to *talk?*" the sorcess asked. The young boys didn't move or say anything. "You will talk! Or you will die, using my new and improved *torture* system!" the queen yelled. "Guards! Take these boys to the torture chambers!" Five unfamiliar guards unlocked the cells and took the boys by their arms out of the cell and dragged them down the jail corridor. The guards opened a door on the right and threw the boys inside.

The room was dark and smelled damp. In the candlelight, Cedar saw a large chair at one end of the room and a large frame in the middle. "Time for *torture!*" yelled the sorcess, walking into the room. "Which one of you wants to try the *electric chair?*"

"I'll do it!" Cedar said in an odd tone of voice.

"Standing up for your little brother, eh? A respectable thing to do! But still, you will both go through pain. Now, then! Younger one! Go over to the frame. And you! Brave one! Sit on the chair!"

Neither Faten nor Cedar said anything. Suddenly Cedar floated up into the air and quickly sped toward the giant chair. Though he struggled, he was no match for the sorcess's powers. When he was in place, metal bars bolted him to the chair.

The sorcess then raised one of her hands, and electric wires taped themselves onto many parts of Cedar's body. With another flick of her wrist, the sorcess used her magic, and a red button on the electric chair pushed in and then went back out again. All of a sudden, three lights on the top of the chair flashed on and Cedar started shaking uncontrollably and screaming. Then he was motionless and speechless, and his eyes were closed.

"*Cedar!*" Faten yelled.

"Don't worry. Your brother is not dead; he has just passed out. But I will continue to *torture* him if you do not *answer* my questions! The choice is up to you. Give me answers, or let me *kill* your brother!" the sorcess said. Faten knew what he had to do.

"I'll answer!" he yelled loudly.

"Oh, good. I knew you'd understand. Now, then, who sent you?"

"Rapid Falls."

"Why?"

"To get food for the village."

"Were you ever with, say...*Aaden?*"

Faten was surprised. How did the sorcess know about Aaden? "Yes."

"What happened to him?"

"He's helping somewhere else."

"*Where?*"

"I—I forgot."

"You'd *better* remember, or else your brother dies."

Faten said, "Alpha Capa...I think."

Satisfied, the sorcess walked over to Cedar and shook him. "Where am I?" he stammered when his eyes opened.

"You're in the evil castle! Don't you remember, brother?" Faten asked.

"Oh yeah...I think I remember this place. What happened to me?" Cedar asked.

"The sorcess—I mean the queen—electrified you!" Faten said.

"How *dare* you call me anything but a queen?" the sorcess yelled. "You two! Follow me!" She led them through the hallway into a large courtyard, where a dragon sat.

"Get onto the tail!" the sorcess yelled, pointing to the dragon. Cedar and Faten walked over to the dragon and grabbed onto its tail. The sorcess levitated off the ground and onto the back of the dragon. "Fly, you stupid animal! Fly to the Omega Sea!" The dragon flapped its wings and lifted off into the air.

Cedar started feeling queasy. "Why do we have to ride on the tail?" he whispered.

"I don't know, but it's to late to jump off. We're already above water." Cedar looked down and saw a vast blue shimmering stretching out beneath them.

"Left! Go *left!*" the sorcess yelled.

"Hey! I have an idea! See that island over there? Let's yell for the dragon to go in that direction and then we can jump off," Cedar said. Faten nodded. "One, two, three...*right!*" both of the boys yelled. The dragon jerked right and the sorcess looked back and saw the boys falling toward the water near a small island.

"Follow them!" she yelled.

"She's coming after us!" Cedar yelled as loud as he could while swimming toward shore.

"When she gets near us, duck underwater. She might give up in a little bit!" Faten yelled. The dragon swooped down, and on cue, Cedar and Faten held their breath and ducked. Faten watched as big feet with sharp nails bobbed in and out of the water, in different places each time. Cedar felt a jerk and was pulled up and dropped onto the island with the sorcess.

"Find the other one!" she yelled to her dragon, and the animal obeyed.

Faten thought they had given up, and he went up for air. Before he knew what was happening, sharp nails pierced the skin on his shoulders and he was lifted into the air and then dropped on hot sand. Faten and Cedar both yelped in pain.

"That should teach you two a lesson!" the sorcess yelled. "Now take your places!" Cedar and Faten slowly got up and grabbed onto the dragon's tail with all their might, and the dragon lifted off.

"*Dive!*" the sorcess yelled once they were over a fairly large island. When they got closer, Cedar saw a large village with many people walking around it. "*Land!*" the sorcess yelled. The massive dragon lightly landed on squishy moss. A villager walked up to Cedar and Faten.

"Oh, I must take you to the nurse," he said. He took the boys by the arms and led them away before the sorcess could say anything.

"Do you happen to know where Aaden is?" the sorcess politely asked a villager walking past.

"You mean the water boy?" he asked.

"I guess so," the sorcess replied, puzzled.

"He is resting now, in that tent. Do not wake the water boy right now." At that, the villager left.

"Stay here, Drack! I have business to take care of!" the sorcess yelled to her dragon, as it followed her to Aaden's tent.

"Hello, Aaden," the sorcess said. Aaden awoke with a start.

"Who are you?" he asked.

"That is not important now. Who sent you here?"

"Why do you want to know?" Aaden asked suspiciously.

"*Just tell me!*" the sorcess yelled.

"I said, why do you want to know?"

"How about this, you so-called magic genius? I'll face you in a magic duel. If you win, I'll give you lots of gold. If I win, you'll answer all of my questions and do whatever I say for two days."

"No," Aaden said simply.

"I'll give you my castle and all of my power and I'll leave you alone."

"No."

"If you don't, I'll *kill* all of the villagers."

Aaden thought about this. "Fine," he said.

"I thought you'd come around. Follow me outside!" the sorcess yelled. Aaden obeyed, slowly walking out of his room and into the open air. When he was outside, Aaden saw many villagers in a circle.

The sorcess turned around so she was facing Aaden. She jerked her hand forward. Aaden felt a strong gust of wind, which knocked him headfirst onto the ground. Before the sorcess had a chance to do another spell, he jumped back up.

"*Alama kalaza!*" he yelled, summoning the sword. The sorcess made a weird motion with her hands, and the sword disappeared. With another jerk of her hands, Aaden was covered in a thin layer of ice.

The sorcess laughed loudly. "Let me get some water while you heat up!" she yelled. She walked over to a barrel and bent down to drink.

"I wouldn't do that if I were you!" a villager yelled, but it was too late. The sorcess had taken a sip of the contaminated water, and she fell to the ground, moaning.

"Water boy!" the crowd cheered.

When Aaden thawed out, he felt weak from the battle and fell to the ground. "Wake up, water boy!" some people yelled.

Aaden stood up and walked over to the barrel he had filled up several times. He had an idea. He walked over to a large area where there were no trees. "*Alcrad!*" he yelled. A hole formed on the ground. "*Alcrad!*" Aaden continued to yell. In a few minutes, the hole covered almost all of the open space.

"*Arogan!*" he yelled. A little bit of water flowed peacefully into the hole out of thin air. "*Arogan! Arogan! Arogan! Arogan!*" Aaden yelled until he was too tired to continue, and the large hole was almost filled with water. Aaden walked to his room and opened the door. He slowly walked over to his bed, and fell asleep before he hit it.

~   ~   ~

"Water boy! Water boy!" some kids yelled happily, running into Aaden's room.

"What?" Aaden said drowsily.

"The animals! They're here! Around the water hole!" a boy yelled. Aaden smiled. His plan had worked! Just then, Shonaia walked into the room, carrying a wooden plate with a chicken wing on it.

"You deserve this," she said, walking over to Aaden and handing him the plate. Aaden picked up the chicken and took a bite. Normally, he wouldn't have liked it that much, but after his hard work, it tasted delicious. Just then, Aaden heard a loud roar. He walked outside and saw a large dragon roaring.

It must be that evil woman's, he said to himself. He walked over to the animal. "You're free!" Aaden yelled. The dragon smiled faintly and lifted off into the sky.

"Aaden!" somebody yelled. Aaden turned around and saw Cedar and Faten running toward him.

"Cedar! Faten! Where have you been?" he yelled.

"We were helping out on another island when an evil sorcess who calls herself a queen caught us. She came here for you. Have you seen her?" Faten said.

"Oh, yeah. She wanted to know who sent me here, but I wouldn't tell her, and then we had a duel, and when she froze me, she drank contaminated water and passed out," Aaden replied.

"Huh, that's handy. Where's Harlume?" Cedar asked.

"I'm not sure. What will you do now?" Aaden said, unfazed. He was used to Harlume's travels.

"I guess we could stay here. You know, since we don't have a way to get back," Faten said.

"Well, the village is low on water and food. I made a watering hole for the animals, so you can help the villagers round them up," Aaden said. Cedar and Faten smiled at each other.

"That would be good job for us," Cedar said.

"Okay. The woman over there helped me get started, and I'm sure she'll give you guys some ideas," Aaden said, pointing at Shonaia.

"Okay," Faten said.

Aaden rested for a while and then went back out to help with the water.

"*Arogan!*" Aaden yelled. A surprising amount of water flowed into the barrel, but Aaden felt more tired than ever. "*Arogan! Arogan! Arogan!*" he yelled.

Suddenly he heard a huge roar.

Aaden turned around and saw a huge animal bounding toward him. It had four wings and sharp claws. Its head swiveled around and had a large eye in the center. Aaden was getting tired, but he concentrated as hard as he could on the beast. "*Alama kalaza!*" he yelled. "*Alama kalaza! Alama kalaza!*" Three swords made of mist stabbed at the animal, one in its heart, one on its legs, and the final one in its eye.

"*Whiiiii!*" the beast yelled as it fell to the ground, and the swords disappeared.

Roaring loudly, four more of the beasts leaped toward Aaden. "*Alama...Alama...Alama...Alama kalaza!*" Aaden yelled. A giant sword of mist stabbed the animals in their eyes and subdued them.

"Are you okay?" Faten asked, running up to Aaden.

"Yeah. I'm fine."

"What happened?" Cedar asked as he arrived.

"It was nothing. I just killed some animals," Aaden said. A few villagers ran up to the animals and pulled them into a large hut.

Roaring, two more of the beasts came out of nowhere and ran toward Aaden. But this time, Aaden was too tired to use a spell, too tired to move, and too tired to call for help. He thought they were surely done for. Suddenly something green from the sky streaked to the scene and knocked out the animals, just in time. "Harlume! You saved me!" Aaden yelled with his leftover strength, when he realized who had saved the day.

~   ~   ~

Aaden found himself in his room looking up at a wood ceiling. *What happened?* he thought, but then it all came back to him.

Those evil beasts running toward him, having no strength left, and Harlume saving his life.

Somebody yelled from outside, interrupting his recollection. Aaden slowly got out of bed and walked toward the commotion. He heard laughter from inside a large hut. Aaden walked inside and saw about twenty people in a room, sitting at a table.

"Water boy. You're well. Why don't you have a bite to eat before you go back to sleep?" Shonaia said from the crowd. Aaden walked to the table and sat down next to Cedar and Faten.

"Why are we eating here?" he asked Cedar.

"I think we're celebrating the great strides we've made to help the village," Cedar replied.

"This food tastes horrible!" Faten said.

"You'll get used to it," Aaden said as he took a bite of meat. After eating and visiting with his friends for a while, Aaden felt tired again. He went to his room and lay down. He left his door open so he could listen to the village sounds. He started to doze off.

Aaden's senses forced him to open his eyes. In the dark, he scanned the room for what had woken him up. He noticed the slightest pressure on his shoulder and felt parchment. Aaden picked it up and saw that it was a map. He yawned and turned on the oil lamp next to his bed. What was more, there was a cut on his neck where the sharp point of the parchment had apparently poked him. It wasn't too bad though, so he looked at the map. It showed Dragondaire and Grutch near the top and the Frosty Mountains in the east. In the south there was the Halder Desert, which Aaden hated to think about. Running between the Halder Desert and the Frosty Mountains was the Omega Sea, with two islands in it labeled Rapid Falls and Alpha Capa. In the middle of the west, the map showed Death Row, and in the middle of that horrid place there was a bubble shape labeled *Forgotten Castles*. Aaden had always wanted to go there, but people kept telling him that few people had ever gotten past Death Row and that a young boy like him didn't have a chance. He had heard from the storytellers that gold lined the streets there, and precious jewels lay everywhere. They said there was an eternal spring there, and flowers bloomed all year.

He looked back at the map. On the top, near the northeast corner were the words *Gateway to the Gatelands*. Nothing was known about that place; nobody who went in came out again. Aaden thought that behind the giant rock gate there might be graveyards and ghosts everywhere, but no one knew for sure. In the north, between Grutch and Dragondaire, he saw the Northern Woods, which ran east until they hit the Frosty Mountains. The woods were home to many animals; people from all over came to hunt them. Touching the Northern Woods, Death Row, the Halder Desert, and the Omega Sea was Ciliagus, the most populated and civilized area in all the land. Ciliagus was also known as the city of trade, for people from Dragondaire, Grutch, and the Northern Woods went there to trade their goods for gold and other things. Ciliagus had the only safe harbor for ships coming from the Omega Sea, and had the largest army. Aaden looked at the Halder Desert, the Omega Sea, and the Frosty Mountains. He remembered when he'd had to cross the Halder with Harlume, but he didn't remember having to cross the Omega Sea to get to the Frosty Mountains. *Curious*, he thought, and pocketed the map.

At about seven-thirty, Aaden woke up and smelled the fresh air. He walked outside to a barrel to make his morning water delivery. "*Arogan!*" he yelled. As usual, some water poured into the barrel. "*Arogan!*" More water. As Aaden continued the process, he noticed that the water was appearing in larger quantities. This happened every time, but today the progress was quite remarkable. It only took about six spells to fill the barrel. Unfortunately, Aaden became very tired, so he walked back into his hut and went back to sleep.

"Water boy!" someone yelled. Aaden opened his eyes. "There's a pack of lions coming! This is our chance. I bet they can feed the whole village!" As Aaden looked closely, he saw that the speaker was Shonaia. "Come on! Before they leave," Shonaia said. Aaden got out of bed as quickly as he could and walked outside. A little bit ahead of him, heading toward the watering hole, were about six or seven golden lions. What looked like all of the people of the village were standing a safe distance away from the animals.

"*Alama kalaza!*" Aaden yelled. As the green sword sped toward the lions, they turned their heads and leapt toward Aaden, and incidentally toward the sword. The villagers yelled as they scattered in all directions. One, two, three, four, five, and finally all (or so Aaden thought) of the lions died.

"Aaden! *Move!*" somebody yelled. It sounded like Cedar. Quickly, Aaden ducked. A lion leapt over him. Blood spurted from Aaden's shoulder and he fell in pain, yelping.

"Fire!" somebody yelled. *Pling! Pling! Pling! Brling!* Four wood arrows sped toward the lion. The lion cried as it hit the ground.

"Move in!" somebody yelled. Shonaia and two other villagers scurried over to Aaden and helped him into a small hut, where he was placed on a bed.

"Don't worry, now. It's all going to be okay," the nurse said to Aaden. "This might hurt a little, but you'll be fine." She pulled out a bottle and pushed the top part down. A mist of water came down on Aaden's cut.

"Ow!" Aaden yelped, forgetting to act brave. The nurse wrapped a long piece of cloth around the wet cut.

"You're going to stay here for the night, okay? Do you want me to let your friends in?" the nurse asked. Aaden nodded. The nurse walked over to the door and opened it. Faten and Cedar came in, and after them Harlume poked his head through the door.

"Are you okay, Aaden?" Cedar asked.

"Yeah, I'm fine," Aaden replied. He wasn't sure if he was lying or not.

"Do you hurt?" Faten asked.

"A little bit, but don't worry," Aaden said. "Harlume, where have you been?" Harlume raised his claws and mimed fighting something. Aaden knew his dragon meant that he had been hunting. Just then, a thought came out of nowhere into Aaden's head. "Rederin! We've been so busy that I haven't thought about him in days!" he said.

"Oh, yeah," Faten said.

"Do you think we should find the pickled willow thingy right now? Or stay and help more here?" Cedar asked.

"We should find the pickled willow. None of us knows how long Rederin has left," Aaden said, getting out of bed. "Let's go tell Shonaia that we'll be back in a while."

When she heard the news, Shonaia said, "Oh, all right. I guess we'll be able to manage for a little while without your help. But do hurry!"

"Bye, Shonaia!" the three yelled as they walked toward Harlume, who apparently knew what was happening and was waiting on the beach.

"You're going to have to carry some extra weight, Harlume," Aaden said to his dragon. Harlume nodded and bent down. Aaden climbed on, followed by Faten and then Cedar. "Hang on, guys!" Aaden yelled as Harlume beat his wings and flew into the open air.

Later, Aaden looked down and saw the massive harbor of Ciliagus. Behind it there were many towers, and he could see people walking all around. Somewhere near the center of town there was a giant castle made of stone. It looked magnificent.

"Look at that," Faten said pointing at the castle.

"Pretty big," Cedar said.

"I hope they don't start shooting arrows at us," Cedar said. Aaden nodded in agreement. In a little while, they were flying over tall green trees and moss.

Somewhere in the center of the Northern Woods, where everything seemed gray and gloomy and where pickled willow bark grew, Harlume dove. Once they were under the canopy of the trees, everyone began to feel cold and gloomy. *Squish!* Harlume landed on the moss. Aaden and the others slid down Harlume's left side onto the ground. "You might want to stay close, Harlume. We might need you," Aaden said.

"Do you know what the pickled willow stuff looks like?" Faten asked.

"I think I've seen it before. It's green and has fuzz in some places. The whole tree is like that. They're easy to spot," Cedar replied.

"Uh, guys, does anyone remember where the oracle lives?" Aaden asked.

"Wasn't he somewhere near here?" Faten said.

"Oh, yeah, I remember," Cedar said.

As he continued walking with Harlume by his side, Aaden felt as though someone were watching him. "Do you feel like someone's watching us?" he asked.

"Yeah. I was just about to ask you the same thing," Cedar said.

"Uh huh," Faten said. Just then, Aaden heard something scurry away.

"Did you hear that?" Cedar and Faten said at the same time.

"Yeah. I think somebody really is following us," Aaden said. Aaden heard something from a tree in front of them. *Swoosh!* A brown net dropped from a tree and pinned Aaden, Cedar, Faten, and Harlume to the ground.

"What the—?" Faten said. Just then, a few boys jumped down from the tree. Harlume instinctively bit at the ropes until there was a large hole, and flew out. The Aader followed quickly.

"Just our luck!" one of the boys said.

"Tell your dragon to back off!" another boy said.

"Or else!" a different boy said.

Whiz! Whiz! Whiz! Whiz! Four arrows shot out of nowhere and hit the attackers, who fell on the ground.

"Who saved us?" Faten asked.

"Not a clue," Aaden said.

"Wait a minute! Is that…pickled willow?" Cedar said excitedly, pointing a finger at a tree in the distance. Aaden whipped his head around and saw a fuzzy green tree. He ran over to it and pulled off a strip of bark.

"Come on!" Aaden said. "We need to get to the oracle." Aaden set a quick pace and was almost running. Cedar and Faten had a hard time keeping up.

"You're sure we're going the right way, right, Aaden?" Faten asked.

"Pretty sure. Hey, Harlume, can you fly ahead and see if you can see the oracle's house?" Aaden said. Harlume nodded and sped forward out of sight.

"Aaden, can you teach us some magic, in case we run into another set of boys, and arrows don't come out of nowhere and save us?" Faten asked.

"Sure," Aaden replied. "You know the *vater wret* spell, right?" Cedar and Faten nodded. "Okay, then. On the count of three, say it at the same time and concentrate on that tree," Aaden said, pointing at a large oak.

"One, two, three! *Vater wret!*" they all yelled. Three strands of blue light, two small and one large, shot out and met in a blue ball in front of the oak. The ball sped forward and hit the tree. A small covering of ice spread across the trunk. "Wow!" Cedar and Faten said.

"Good job!" Aaden said. Just then, Harlume came through an opening between two trees. He pointed his left wing forward, urgently. Then he bent down.

"Let's ride Harlume for a bit," Aaden said, climbing on. Cedar followed, and then Faten. Harlume beat his wings and rose into the air again. To Aaden, it felt like his dragon was flying much faster than usual. And in no time at all, Aaden found Harlume diving toward a wooden house. "This is it!" he said as Harlume lightly landed.

Rap tap tap. Cedar knocked on the door. Aaden heard foot-steps, and then the oracle opened the door, "You have come once more, young ones," he said, as if only a few hours had passed since they had left him.

"We have found the pickled willow bark, sir," Aaden said.

"Oh, good. Here, step inside, and I'll prepare the potion," the ora-cle said, stepping out of the doorway. The boys walked anxiously inside, and Harlume stayed outside. They found Rederin lying in one corner, as if sleeping. In another corner there was a large brown pot next to a counter. Aaden pulled the bark out of his pocket and gave it to the oracle, who took it and walked to the pot. The oracle opened a cupboard above the counter and pulled out two bottles of purple and orange liquid. He pulled off the corks and then dumped the bottles into the pot. Then he put in the bark and stirred the potion with his hand. When he finished, he brought the pot over to Rederin, bringing along a large wooden spoon. With help from Faten, he moved Rederin's head up so that he could spoon some of the liquid into his mouth. In a moment, Aaden's best friend opened his eyes.

"Aaden! Cedar! Faten! Is that you?" he said. "The dream. I had a dream. There was blackness. I was stuck in the blackness. There was a white spot in the distance. I tried to get to it. I never did," Rederin said.

The others were relieved that he had awakened, but were con-cerned about his well-being.

"This behavior can be expected. He may seem disoriented for a while, but soon he should be back to normal. He will probably be asking you guys a lot of questions. You can rest here until he's ready to leave," the oracle said.

The group proceeded to answer Rederin's questions, and they did their best to briefly tell him about the adventures that had hap-pened while he was unconscious. To their relief, he began to sound like his old self, though he was pretty amazed at what they had been up to without him. Together, they decided they should return to their duties as soon as possible. They would tell Rederin more on their way.

"We can't thank you enough for all your help. I wish we had some way to pay," Aaden said.

"Don't worry about it. I'm happy I could help," the oracle said as the Aader walked out the door.

"Thanks again! Bye!" the Aader called back.

"You can go hunt, Harlume. I think we should probably walk instead of riding you. Four people might be a little too heavy," Aaden said. Harlume nodded and flew into the air, and the boys resumed their conversation.

Rederin said, "I had a really weird dream that lasted for a long time. It seemed like it was months. I was trapped in black swirls. I couldn't get to the white. It was really scary. The black swirls were everywhere." He closed his eyes. "I still can't believe all those things you told me. You did all that? While I was sleeping?"

The rest of the boys nodded.

"And where did you say Drakint is?" Rederin asked.

"Well, you see, Faten and I were chased by a lion when we were hunting for Rapid Falls. We wound up in an evil castle, and there was a lady there who called herself a queen. She tortured me with an electric chair until we told her where Aaden was, so we told her and then we went with her to Alpha Capa. But then she fought with Aaden," Cedar said.

"I didn't *defeat* her; she just drank some toxic water from the smire and died," Aaden interrupted.

"Yeah, okay, but anyway, that's why Drakint is still at Rapid Falls," Cedar finished.

"I can't believe you guys went to the Dragonriders'—" Rederin began, but stopped.

In front of the group was a ten-foot-high wall of mist, which seemed to stretch on forever.

"Should we keep going?" Faten asked with more than a hint of worry in his voice.

"We could," Cedar said.

"It's just mist. What could go wrong?" Rederin said.

"I think I've heard about this place before. Somewhere, but I just can't remember what it was. Oh, well. Since Harlume isn't here to check it out, we should probably go," Aaden said, and the Aader walked into the wall of mist.

"Death Row!" the group screamed. In front of them was a narrow stream of water, running forward into the distance. Around the water there were flowers blooming, and everything seemed very peaceful and relaxed. To the left of the stream there was a large plain that looked like a desert, with many suns all around. To the right of the stream there were large mountains with hail and snow crashing down on them. In the distance, everywhere except in the line of the stream, there were lumps lying around that appeared to be bodies.

"We found the stream!" Cedar yelled. The books Aaden had read about Death Row had mentioned its horrid temperatures, and the one stream that flowed right through the middle and led straight to the Forgotten Castles, where there was perfect weather.

"I don't believe it!" Aaden yelled.

"Come on, guys! Let's hurry to the Forgotten Castles," Faten said excitedly.

Chapter 9

"*Wow!*" the Aader yelled. In front of them were five stone castle-like mansions. Around them were marble streets covered in gold and jewels.

"What are we going to do with all of this?" Faten asked.

"Maybe we can make a gold and jewel refinery," Rederin said.

"Yeah. So we can make a wagon and haul all the gold and stuff to it," Cedar said.

"But we can't forget where the stream is," Aaden said.

"There's a tree over there. Let's build the wagon!" Faten said, pointing to a brown tree.

"With what?" Cedar asked.

"There might be some axes in the castles," Aaden said.

"There should be some," Rederin said. The Aader walked to the door of the castle closest to them. Rederin pulled it open.

"Wow!" Faten said. Inside they saw a giant table that stretched to the end of the room. Along it were hundreds of wooden chairs with people sitting on them. At the head of the table was a man dressed in a red velvet robe with a white fur lining; a golden crown was on his head. Next to him was a woman dressed in similar clothes, wearing a silver crown on her head. She was also wearing three gold necklaces bearing different stone pendants, and a few sparkling gold bracelets. The boys initially stood dumbfounded, but soon realized that the people in the room had been frozen in place by some sorcery. Slowly, they relaxed and remembered their plan.

"Look! There's an axe in the corner," Aaden said, but his friends were staring at the king's and queen's crowns and jewels.

"I call the king's crown!" Faten yelled.

"I call the queen's!" Rederin yelled.

"I'll take the queen's jewelry," Cedar said.

"Guys! We didn't come in here to get gold and jewels! Come on! It could be dangerous to touch these people. And don't forget what happened the last time we stole something. Let's look for more tools," Aaden said. Nonetheless, as they walked to the axe, Rederin, Faten, and Cedar took the jewelry they had claimed.

"Does anyone want to start cutting wood? Or should we find four axes first?" Aaden asked.

The other boys looked at each other and said nothing.

"There's probably more in the armory," Rederin said, pointing to a door that read *ARMORY* in gold letters.

"Yeah," Cedar replied. Faten pulled open the door, and they walked inside.

It was a small room with swords, spears, arrows, bows, axes, and all kinds of weapons hanging from the ceiling or leaning against the walls. In the corners and in the middle were eight suits of armor, each complete with a helmet, sword, and shield. The Aader walked over to the axes and each took one.

"Now that we have our axes, let's go chop wood," Rederin said.

"Let's look in the treasury!" Faten said.

"How 'bout we do that after we make a wagon and a refinery?" Aaden replied.

"That will take forever!" Faten said.

"Okay. We'll explore after we make the wagon," Aaden said. With greedy thoughts, they chopped wood as fast as they could.

"You think this is enough?" Cedar said. In an hour, the group had chopped a total of ten small logs, and they were beginning to tire.

"Yeah. But how are we going to put them together? There aren't any nails here," Faten said.

"I saw some in the armory and put a bunch in my pockets. See?" Cedar said, showing them some nails. The others were pleased at his forethought.

"First we need to put four big pieces together and make a frame. Cedar and Faten can start that. Rederin, you can chop some more wood for the wagon floor. I'll think about wheels. And try to make it big!" Aaden said, grabbing a pickaxe and a piece of wood.

Chop! Rederin threw his axe against a tree, Cedar and Faten hit the nails with pickaxes, and Aaden hit the center of a rectangular piece of wood.

Soon they had a large wooden frame supported by four wheels, and in the frame there sat a large tub they had found in a building nearby.

"Now let's load in the gold!" Cedar said. The Aader spread out into the streets and picked up as much gold and as many jewels as they could hold before dumping it into the tub and gathering more.

It was about five minutes later when the Aader had filled up the tub completely. They gathered around it.

"Let's go the same way we came from, so we'll get to the Northern Woods. There are plenty of trees there we can use to make a refinery," Aaden said.

"Once we get out of Death Row, how are we supposed to know where the stream is?" Faten asked. The group thought for a moment.

"Oh, I know!" Rederin said. "One person can stay near the stream, and then once everything's ready, somebody in the woods can hold a stick out into the cloud, and then the person still in Death Row can tell the others which way to go," Rederin said as the group began walking.

"But who would stay in Death Row for that long?" Cedar asked.

"We can just dump out the gold and stuff and then come back for more," Aaden said.

"Don't you think somebody should guard the gold while we're getting more?" Rederin asked.

"We can split into two groups," Aaden said. "Two people can guard while the other two are getting more. Once we get a bunch of jewels and gold, three of us can work on the refinery and the other person can stay in Death Row. We can switch places frequently."

Aaden and Rederin dumped out the jewels and the tools as Faten and Cedar waited behind the cloud wall. Aaden picked up a stick and stuck it into the cloud. Nothing happened.

"Cedar! Faten! Where are you?" Rederin yelled. No answer.

"The wall must have a spell on it so that no sound can get through," Aaden mused.

"Then what are we supposed to do?" Rederin asked.

"I have an idea, but it might be dangerous," Aaden said bluntly.

"What?" Rederin asked. But Aaden didn't answer. Instead he stuck the stick into the cloud once more. Then, with the end of the stick touching his chest, he stepped into the cloud. All around him was impenetrable mist. He looked down to his right. Careful not to move the stick, he stepped back into the Northern Woods.

"Follow me," he said. Rederin shivered.

Rederin walked over to him. Aaden walked back into the cloud and looked back. He saw Rederin standing behind him. He tried to say "See, everything's fine" but no noise came out. He pushed the stick further in and walked forward. Then he pushed the stick forward once more. There was a rustling noise, and then a stick popped out in front of Aaden. He walked forward and out of the mist.

"What took you so long?" Faten asked.

"Well, first we stuck a stick into the mist, but we didn't hear you answer, so we went into the mist, which was much bigger than I remembered it, and Aaden stuck a stick in," Rederin answered.

"Oh. Well, we'll guard while you get more treasure. I'll go back into the wood and bring the wagon," Cedar said.

"Make sure you stay next to the part of the cloud that you came in through!" Aaden called before Faten and Cedar walked to the other side of the cloud.

Soon, Faten stepped back out of Death Row, pulling the wagon.

"Here," he said, pushing the wagon over to them.

"Thanks," Rederin said.

"While you're waiting for us, you can start chopping logs for the refinery," Aaden said.

"Okay. Bye!" Faten said as he stepped back into the cloud.

Rederin grabbed the handle of the wagon and the two began walking toward the castles in the distance. "I'm tired of walking back and forth. Hey, what are we going to do with our riches anyway?" he said.

"We need to use it to help our friends," Aaden replied.

"Maybe we can buy some land and build an empire and…and…start a revolution or something!" Rederin said.

"Possibly. But we probably don't have enough gold to do that," Aaden said. "Wait a minute. Shouldn't we be helping Alpha Capa and Rapid Falls?"

"Hey! Why don't we ship all of the gold and stuff to the islands?" Rederin said excitedly.

"That's not a bad idea. We can build some sort of a rail system to the Omega Sea, and then we can ship supplies to the islands. That would help them more than just hunting animals and giving them fresh water," Aaden said.

"And we could call it the GTG, for Gold Transportation Group," Rederin said.

"Or the Gold Transportation Company!" Aaden said.

"Or the Gold Transportation Agency," Rederin said. Aaden looked ahead and saw the end of the stream, and the gold-filled streets of the Forgotten Castles beyond.

"We're here already?" Aaden said.

"That was quick!" Rederin said. They both bent down and picked up a bunch of gold, using their shirts as bags, and carried the gold back to the wagon.

"Hey, I don't remember that place before," Rederin said, looking at a small building next to one of the castles.

"Do you want to go in?" Aaden said.

"Sure," Rederin replied, and they walked up to the door of the building. Aaden pushed it open. They saw a dark room with a few candles flickering on the walls. In the back, the room was filled with jars stacked on top of each other; the jars were filled with black liquid. "What's all that stuff?" Rederin asked.

"Wait—I think my dad told me about these before. Oh, yeah! It's *graete!*" Aaden said, excited to have remembered.

"*Graete?*" Rederin asked.

"You know, that rare stuff that's found buried really far underground—and it's even very valuable! It's supposed to make machines move really fast. Maybe it will help us with our projects."

Beginning or Ending

Is this the beginning
Of a new life,
Or the end of an old?
Beginning to use
New arrows,
Or Ending to use
The others?
Begin a
New job,
But keep in mind
What you're doing
To the other.
Beginning or ending...
You be the judge.

Chapter 10

"Let's load the rest of our wagon with *graete*, if it's as valuable as you say," Rederin said.

"Okay, but it's supposed to be really heavy," Aaden said. They walked over to the bottles, and each picked one up.

"Wow!" Rederin said as he tilted to one side from the weight. Aaden almost fell over, but quickly regained his balance and put the bottle into the wagon. Rederin did the same. Aaden tried pulling the wagon.

"It's pretty heavy already, so we can just take this much for now," he said. Rederin walked over and pulled it a little bit.

"Yeah, you're right. Do you mind pulling this time?" he asked.

"No," Aaden said.

As the two walked out of the room and toward the stream, Rederin said, "I wonder what Drakint's doing right now. I wonder if he's still doing good deeds."

Aaden thought about the time Drakint had taken coins from Rederin. He tried to get rid of the uncomfortable memory by saying, "Did we tell you about what happened the first time we tried to find pickled willow bark?"

"Oh, yeah. I remember. What happened, again?" Rederin said.

"Well, to make a long story short, we were captured and thrown in jail. Somehow we all managed to escape. But then we were chased by armies, and then rescued by the dragonriders' school," Aaden reminded him.

"What was it like...the Dragonriders' Academy?" Rederin asked. Aaden thought about the time he had spent taking classes, and about the wars.

"First we just took a bunch of classes: magic, horseback riding, sword fighting, and we had an archery class with an incompetent teacher. But I learned some magic, and then I accidentally did a spell, and then Mr. Ponn—"

"Who's Mr. Ponn?" Rederin interrupted.

"Oh, he's the head of the academy. He's the one who sent us out to do good deeds. So anyway, he needed my help, so for a while I just took private magic lessons with him. And then there was a war, and Mr. Ponn and the magic teacher and I threw spells at the enemies from a balcony. After the war, I was sent to get the Ruishi Crystal, but it wasn't there, so then me and Harlume followed these boys who happened to have just stolen the Ruishi Crystal, and then I, well, um, knocked them out and brought the crystal back to Mr. Ponn. But when we got there the school was in the middle of another war, and there were all these little snake things. Mr. Ponn took me to a tower, and I put the Ruishi Crystal on an altar."

"But how come you left for Alpha Capa?" Rederin asked.

"Faten and Cedar and I had a weird dream that showed us stealing horses, and then the war that we lost," Aaden said.

"You lost the war?" Rederin asked.

"Oh...yeah," Aaden said. He had forgotten to mention that little detail.

"Well, go on!" Rederin demanded.

"We thought maybe we had caused the dragonriders to lose the war because of our stealing the horses, so we decided to go help people to make up for it," Aaden said.

"Look!" Rederin said, pointing at the front of the mist ahead of them. Sticking out from the mist was a wooden stick. Letting go of the wagon, Aaden ran to the spot and lightly pushed the stick forward. The stick disappeared. Rederin ran up to Aaden, and they walked into the mist and through it into the woods.

"What took you so long?" Faten said.

"Huh?" was Rederin's reply.

"You were gone for hours!" Faten said. Rederin and Aaden looked at each other.

"We must have gotten so caught up in talking that we walked really slowly," Aaden said.

Rederin looked beyond Faten at a giant pile of chopped wood and said, "How did you chop so much wood?"

"Like Faten said, you guys took forever," Cedar said.

"Oh, yeah—when we were getting gold, we went into a building, and it was filled with *graete,* so we took some with us," Aaden said.

"*Graete?*" Faten and Cedar exclaimed. Rederin nodded.

"We can make a railway car that's powered by the *graete,*" Rederin said as he cleared out the wagon.

"Oh, that sounds interesting," Faten said.

"Aaden and I had an idea," Rederin began. "Well, you know how you guys were helping the islands? Don't you think it would be best if we shipped the gold to them? Then we can return to the school," he said.

"Hey! That's a great idea!" Faten said.

"But how?" Cedar asked."

"You know all of the tales about *graete* and how it can power something and make it go really fast? We can make a vehicle and use the *graete* to power it," Aaden said.

"Oh," Cedar said, sounding a little confused.

"But wouldn't it be way too much work to build something that runs all the way to the Omega Sea?" Faten said.

"How would we control it?" Cedar asked.

"Good question," Rederin said, pondering.

Aaden thought for a moment and then said, "Maybe a track could run from the refinery."

"Hey, Rederin? Didn't you say your dad built machines that could use *graete*?" Cedar asked.

"Uh huh. Dad showed me how to make a machine like that," Rederin said.

"I never knew that," Aaden said.

"Me neither," Faten said.

"Is it hard?" Cedar asked.

"No, it's actually really easy," Rederin replied.

"Well, it'll take us forever to build a track," Faten said.

"Don't you think we should make the refinery first?" Cedar said.

"Yeah," Rederin said.

"How about we set things up in a clearing?" Faten said.

"Okay," Aaden said. "Do any of you know of a good location?"

"I think I remember one," Cedar said, turning around and walking off. The others followed.

"Is that it?" Rederin said, pointing in front of them.

"Now I see it," Aaden and Faten said together, then looked at each other.

"Let's roll the logs over there," Rederin said. The Aader all went over to the pile of lumber and began rolling it to the clearing.

"That's the last one," Faten said as he rolled the last of the logs into the clearing.

"We're probably going to need a lot of long nails," Cedar said.

"And some more people," Rederin said.

"You think?" Aaden said. They nodded.

"I have an idea! Why don't we go to Dragondaire and use some of the gold to buy supplies?" Faten suggested.

Aaden heard something and looked up. He saw Harlume darting down toward them, and he waved his arms. The rest of the Aader looked up. "I forgot all about him," Cedar said.

"Aaden, do you think he could carry a sack of gold?" Rederin asked.

"Probably," Aaden replied as Harlume carefully landed in front of them.

"But we don't have any sacks. Well, just small ones," Faten said.

"We could go back to the oracle, if any of you remember how," Aaden said.

"Didn't we just come from over there?" Rederin asked, pointing backward to the right.

"We might as well try," Aaden said. "Harlume, how many of us do you think you can carry without hurting yourself?" Harlume beat his wings three times and then stopped.

"I don't mind walking by myself, as long as you guys are near," Rederin said.

"Really?" Aaden asked. Rederin nodded. "Harlume will fly slowly over the trees to where Cedar thinks it is. We'll look down occasionally, and if you're not there we'll come down and look for you," Aaden said as he mounted his dragon. Faten and Cedar followed, with difficulty. Aaden remembered the first time he had ridden on Harlume.

"You guys have ridden on Harlume before, right?" he asked.

"Uh huh," Faten and Cedar replied.

As Harlume beat his wings and lifted into the air, Aaden said, "I wonder how Alpha Capa and Rapid Falls are doing."

"Rapid Falls wasn't too bad when we left," Cedar said.

"Yeah, they probably were able to manage okay after we left," Faten chimed in. By now Harlume had risen above the tallest trees and was gliding slowly over them. Aaden looked down at Rederin and waved.

Aaden looked at his timepiece just as Harlume began to dive toward a brown cabin below. It read 4:13. As they landed, Aaden looked behind and saw Rederin. "Have a good walk?" Faten asked.

Rederin nodded. "But is it okay if I ride on the way back?" he asked.

"I'll walk," Cedar said.

"It's okay; I'll do it," Aaden said.

"But Harlume is *your* dragon," Cedar replied.

"Oh, all right," Aaden said. Cedar, Faten, and Aaden dismounted Harlume and walked to Rederin as he knocked on the oracle's door.

"What can I do for you, boys?" the oracle said, welcoming them into his hut.

"We came to get the sack that we left. And do you have a rope we can borrow?" Aaden said.

"Oh, it's over in my bedroom. And I might have a rope in my closet. I'll be right back," the oracle said, walking toward a door.

"Do you need any help?" Rederin asked.

"No, I'll be fine," the oracle replied, opening and walking through the door.

"I think we should let him keep the money, you know, for saving Rederin," Aaden said. The group nodded.

"And besides, we have plenty from the Forgotten Castles," Cedar said.

"The Forgotten Castles! What if we can't find that stream again!" Rederin said frantically. But before anyone could add to that, the oracle walked into the room, carrying the sack.

"Here you go," he said, handing Aaden the sack with a long brown rope on top.

"You can keep the coins; all we need is the sack and the rope," Aaden replied.

The oracle looked surprised and said, "Are you sure? I'm sure you worked very hard to obtain this."

"Oh, we're sure. It will just slow us down, and we are greatly indebted to you for saving Rederin," Aaden said.

"Just one moment," the oracle said, and again walked into his bedroom.

"We left the gold in front of the entrance to the stream, though," Faten said, resuming the conversation. The oracle suddenly walked back into the room carrying a small wooden box.

"I have a gift for you in return for the money," he said. "It has been passed down in my family for many generations, and I know will prove very useful to you." He opened the top of the box, revealing a light blue stone that lit up the entire room.

"It is a *dreále*. To use it, you must first find my brother. He will know how to use it on your dragon, who will be granted the power of speech. If you do not wish your dragon to have the power of speech, many people in Dragondaire will be willing to trade valuables for it. If you decide to use it, my brother lives at the border between Grutch and the Northern Woods. He is the only known living wizard in that area. Well, then, I hope to see you soon," the oracle said, shooing the group out.

Once the oracle had shut the door, Faten said, "I've never heard of a *dreále* before, or of anything that can make a dragon talk."

"So, should we head toward Grutch?" Rederin asked. They all looked at each other.

"Well, I don't really want to waste our time now. Maybe when we're already on our way to Grutch," Aaden said. "Let's go, then," he added. Faten, Rederin and he climbed onto Harlume as Cedar began walking back the way they had come.

"Cedar, meet us next to the mist wall where the gold is!" Faten yelled after him.

"Rederin, do you have any questions before riding Harlume for the first time?" Aaden asked as Harlume began beating his wings.

"Is it scary?" he asked.

"Well, maybe just a little bit the first time, but it's really pretty fun," Aaden replied.

"The best part is when Harlume is gliding straight, and the wind whips your face," Faten said. Aaden nodded in agreement.

Chapter 11

Aaden picked up the sack that the Aader had just filled with gold, gems, and the *dreále*. "We can use the rope to hang it around Harlume's body," Aaden said.

"Oh, so that's what the rope was for," Faten said.

"Can somebody help me? It's a tad on the heavy side," Aaden asked.

"I'll help," Rederin replied, walking over to Aaden and picking up the bottom of the sack.

"How are we going to put the rope through?" he asked.

"The bag came with two holes," Aaden replied, putting the rope through them. "We might need someone else to hold it while I make a knot."

"I'll do it," Cedar said, walking over to Rederin and holding up one side of the bag.

"Let's get it under Harlume," Aaden said. The group bent down as they walked into Harlume's shadow. Aaden climbed onto his dragon.

"Faten, can you hand me the rope?" Aaden said from atop Harlume. Faten walked under Harlume and moved the two ropes around Harlume's body until he felt Aaden grab them. Aaden carefully used the remainder of the rope to make four knots, just to make sure it wouldn't fall off.

"Okay, you guys can let go now," he said to Rederin and Cedar. He felt a drop as they let the sack drop a little lower.

"Raahhr!" Harlume yelled.

"Harlume might only be able to carry two of us at a time. Drag-ondaire's pretty far away, so we should probably take turns walking and riding," Aaden said.

"I can walk," Cedar said.

"I don't mind," Aaden said. "All you have to do is just say 'left,' 'right,' or 'dive,'" he added.

"If you're sure," Rederin said.

"Don't worry. What could happen?" Aaden said. Rederin and Faten climbed onto Harlume. "You'll be fine." Aaden said as Har-lume beat his wings. He and Cedar began walking past Harlume, northward to Dragondaire.

"Aaaaah!" Aaden turned around and saw Harlume just above the trees, shaking about frantically.

"Harlume! What are you doing? Get down here!" Aaden yelled. But it was too late. Harlume had just sent Rederin and Faten tum-bling toward the ground. The dragon flew off into the distance.

"Aaaaah!" Rederin yelled from where he had fallen. He and Faten had fallen hard and were moaning. Aaden and Cedar rushed over as quickly as they could.

When they got closer, Aaden was horrified to see Rederin's back spilling out blood. Aaden put pressure on the wound so the bleed-ing would lessen.

"Here, use this!" Cedar said, shoving a long piece of cloth toward Aaden.

"Where'd you get this?" Aaden asked, laying the cloth around Rederin's back.

"Never mind!" Cedar yelled back, examining Faten.

"Aaaaaah! Stop!" Rederin yelled.

"I'm almost done. Stand up...slowly," Aaden said calmly. Rederin jerked his body up a little bit. "Stay there," Aaden said. He tied the cloth around Rederin's stomach as tightly as he could.

"Ow! Ow! What are you doing!" Rederin yelled.

"Faten's all right. He's just sore and has a few scratches," Cedar said.

~   ~   ~

Days passed slowly as the Aader trudged onward to Dragondaire. Harlume was nowhere in sight.

"I wonder if Harlume will ever turn up here with the gold, because it's pointless to go to Dragondaire with no gold," Faten said.

"I don't remember the Northern Woods being so large. Shouldn't it only have taken about a couple of days?" Rederin asked.

"Are you sure we're going the right way? I don't think I've ever been to this part of the Northern Woods before, and I've been to most parts," Cedar said.

"No! We're not! That's the Gateway!" Aaden said, pointing to a series of rocky mountains leagues in front of them.

"But if we keep going straight into the Gatelands, won't we see Dragondaire?" Aaden asked.

"Oh, yeah. The Gateway touches Dragondaire. It'll just take a lot longer than if we had gone straight to Dragondaire from the stream," Cedar replied.

"I've never been to the Gateway before. My dad forbade it," Rederin said.

"So did mine," Aaden replied.

"Look!" Cedar yelled, pointing at several dots in the sky.

"Duck behind those giant rocks over there!" Aaden yelled. The group dodged a few boulders until they were in the relative safety of some large rocks.

"I bet it's Grutch," Faten whispered, trying to sound tough. The truth was, they were all pretty scared since the last war.

"They're nearer. They've brought dragons; I can hear them," Aaden whispered.

The boys crouched together, shivering.

"They're here somewhere! I saw them!" a voice boomed. The boys almost stopped breathing. Rederin leaned back against one of the boulders, causing a large stone to fall from the top. He reached out to get it, but missed. The rock crashed to the ground.

"Oh, yeah. They're here, all right!" another voice boomed. Aaden heard a few people whispering, and then the sounds of footsteps coming closer.

"*Run!*" Cedar yelled, who had apparently also heard the slow breathing and footsteps of the men. *Pling! Pling! Pling!* Three arrows sped toward the group.

"Get the one in front!" one of the men yelled. Three other men ran toward Aaden with swords in their hands.

"Dragondaire! Over there!" Faten yelled. The group turned right. Rederin slowed down due to his injured back. Out of nowhere, five men covered in armor appeared in front of them. *Pling! Pling! Pling! Pling!* But the arrows weren't aimed at Aaden. They had been shot from the sky; of that, Aaden was sure. The arrows pierced the armor, killing the five men in front of them. Aaden quickly glanced at the sky, but nothing was there. He turned to see his friends running away.

"Aaden! What are you doing? *Run!*" Cedar yelled.

Aaden thought about all he had learned at the school and during his adventures. He would not run away from these men like a coward.

"You go!" he yelled back to his friends, then turned to face the men. To Aaden's surprise, instead of four or five men, there were about thirty of them. "*Alama kalaza!*" he yelled. But there was another voice yelling the same spell at the same time.

The sword was larger than it had ever been before—almost as tall as Aaden. It twirled around in the air with great agility toward the men. Aaden turned around. He saw his friends staring at him, then Faten and Cedar fell to the ground.

"Did you guys do that spell?" he asked Rederin.

Rederin nodded. "How come they fell to the ground?" he asked.

"The spell was too advanced. How did you know how to do it? Not even Dragonmaster Ponn could do that," Aaden said. Rederin shrugged.

"Is that Harlume?" Rederin suddenly asked, pointing at a dragon diving toward them carrying a sack.

"I think it is," Aaden replied.

Harlume quietly landed in front of Aaden. Rederin backed away. The dragon bent down next to Cedar and Faten and licked their faces. They sat up.

"Ah!" they both yelled.

"It's Harlume," Aaden said. "Does anyone want to ride with me?" he added.

"I'll do it," Rederin said.

"Are you sure? Is your back better?" Aaden asked.

"I'm sure," Rederin replied, mounting Harlume's back. Aaden mounted near Harlume's head.

"Fly to Dragondaire. And don't get crazy again!" Aaden said. Harlume made a weird whine before flying into the air.

"Meet you at the Dragondaire castle!" Cedar called after them.

As they approached the castle, Aaden yelled, "Dive! Head toward the castle!" Harlume sent a fireball down in front of them as he dove. When they landed, Cedar and Faten were waiting for them in front of the castle. Harlume had apparently attracted attention with the fireball, for a group of people had gathered around them. Aaden dismounted and walked to one of the guards of the castle. "I'd like to talk to the king. Tell him I have brought gold and want to buy supplies," he said. The guard nodded and disappeared behind the castle door.

Minutes later, a man wearing a red robe and an oversized gold crown walked to Aaden. Around him were four knights wearing silver armor, each carrying a sword. "You wanted to talk?" the king asked.

"Yes, your majesty. But before we discuss trading, would you be so kind as to provide a meal for us? We have not eaten in days," Aaden said.

"Certainly. Guards, take the sack off the dragon and bring it in."

Plates full of all kinds of food crowded the table. There were mashed potatoes, all kinds of meat, apples, pears, chocolates, bread, and Aaden's favorite—green olives. In front of each diner was a plate, two forks, two spoons, a knife, and a goblet, all inlaid with gold. Aaden couldn't help taking a double serving of olives, but nobody seemed to mind. He tried almost everything except the pear, for he was filled by the time he got to the fruit. He had never dined this well before.

"So what was it you wanted in exchange for the gold?" the king asked after the meal.

"Oh, we need some long nails and some trustworthy people to help us," Aaden replied.

"Shall we examine what you have?" the king asked anxiously.

"Certainly," Aaden said, trying to act prestigious.

"Guards! Bring in the sack!" the king yelled. Moments later two guards walked into the room, carrying the sack of gold and gems. The king moved his hand down in an awkward fashion several times. The guards carefully dumped out the gems onto the ground in front of the king.

"Now, how did you come across these things?" he asked.

"Oh, um, we worked for Oodan of Farmlinder, your majesty, for a very long time," Aaden replied.

"And we bought some of the rarer things," Rederin added quickly as the king stared at the *dreále*.

"I'll take these gems, and I'll give you seven knights, seven horses, one hundred nails, and a sack of supplies," the king said, setting aside the *dreále* and about ten other gems.

"How about the same deal with five horses, and I keep the *dreále*?" Aaden suggested. He saw an angry look in the king's eyes.

"Certainly," the king sputtered.

"Trust me, your majesty, you will not regret your decision," Aaden replied.

"Guards, get me seven knights; prepare five horses outside the main gate; fill a bag with one hundred nails and a prepare a bag full of utensils, water, food, and supplies; and take these gems to my quarters," said the king. The guards looked at each other.

"Go!" the king yelled. After they had left, he said, "The knights are very obedient and will prove to be very useful in your travels." Aaden pocketed the *dreále* quickly, but noticed it seemed to lack its usual gleam. He dismissed the thought, however, because he was tired and ready to continue his journey.

"Guards, can you carry these sacks? One of them is full of nails," Aaden asked. They nodded. Aaden handed the sacks to them and whispered to Faten, "Keep an eye on them." Faten nodded and rode his horse up in front of them. Aaden said, "Rederin, you seem to like Harlume. Do you want to ride him?"

"Sure," Rederin replied, mounting Harlume behind Aaden.

"Cedar, you're good with directions. Can you make sure they make it to where the gold is?" Aaden asked.

"Okay," Cedar replied.

"We'll hurry back and get to work. If we're not there when you get there, you can start working on the track," Aaden said. Harlume beat his wings impatiently and lifted into the air.

"Bye!" Cedar yelled.

"Bye!" Aaden and Rederin yelled back.

"Go to where the gold is," Aaden said to Harlume. "You can go as fast as you want," he added. In response, Harlume sped forward.

"Wow! What are those?" Rederin asked, pointing to a group of small yellow animals near the mist wall.

"It's a gathering of Golden Delivery Squice. They only come when someone very important is hurt or if they have important news," Aaden replied. Rederin looked at him suspiciously.

"You've never seen a squice before?" Aaden asked, bewildered.

"No. I've never heard of them before," Rederin replied.

"Dive!" Aaden interrupted, seeing the familiar pile of gold. As the two dismounted, Aaden said, "Did you know that squice were the first animals? All the other animals evolved from them."

"Are you serious?" Rederin asked. Aaden nodded.

"Oh, look. The squice are coming toward us," Aaden said.

"Squice have wings?" Rederin asked.

"Most of them don't. Supposedly, only a few winged ones are left in the world. But there must be hundreds if this many have come to see us," Aaden said. One of the squice scurried up to Aaden, carrying a piece of parchment in its mouth. Aaden reached down and took it out. It read:

Aaden, this message is very important. Alpha Capa is having a dire shortage of water and food. You need to come quickly! The fate of Alpha Capa lies in your hands!
—Shonaia and the people of my tribe

Rederin peered at the note over Aaden's shoulder. "Isn't that the place you helped out?" he asked. Aaden nodded.

"They need my help. I must go. When the Aader and the knights come, tell them Alpha Capa needs me. Tell them to start building the refinery and the track without me. Tell them to keep a close eye on the guards. I must go," Aaden said, remounting Harlume. "Go to the Omega Sea," he said as Harlume flew into the air. "I'll just get them some water and then come back! Don't worry!" he yelled back to Rederin. But little did he know that this trip to Alpha Capa would be very memorable.

Saved

Saved, just saved
Mysteriously,
Nobody knows how
But saved all the same.
There's nothing like it,
Being saved.
That is,
It's like being
Given a great
Present
By somebody
who you used to
Think of as
Rude, unkind,
Not your type.

Chapter 12

"Aaden! You're back! You must hurry. The king awaits your return. Rod! Take this dragon somewhere!" Shonaia urged. Aaden followed her to the middle of the island, where there was a small tower made of wood and stone. A young man walked out the door. His hair was tangled in knots and his leather clothes were torn. He was carrying a basket in his hands.

"Please fill," he said, nodding toward the basket.

Aaden took the basket from him and lay it on the ground. "*Arogan! Arogan!*" he yelled. About a gallon of water filled the basket. Just as Aaden was about to repeat the spell, the man rushed the basket back into the tower.

"Can you fill this cup?" Shonaia asked, holding up half of a coconut shell.

"*Arogan!*" Aaden yelled, trying not to overflow the cup. Just the right amount went in. "Thank you," Shonaia said, and drank the water slowly. Just then, a group of people came over to Aaden, each carrying either two coconut halves or a small barrel. Aaden walked over to the people in front and yelled, "*Arogan! Arogan! Arogan! Arogan!*" into their containers.

"Thank you, water boy!" some of them said before gulping down the water.

"Where is the water supply?" Aaden asked Shonaia.

"Keep going straight ahead for a few minutes and then turn right and you'll see one," Shonaia replied. She disappeared into the happy group of people with their newly quenched thirsts.

Along his way to the water supply, quite a few people came up to Aaden asking for water. Soon Aaden came across the hole he had made the last time he was in Alpha Capa, but now it was almost empty.

"*Arogan! Arogan! Arogan!*" he yelled, filling it halfway. He kept walking until he saw the barrels. "There's more water in the barrels!" he yelled out. "*Arogan! Arogan! Arogan!*" he yelled. The first two spells produced about half a gallon of water, but the third one filled the barrel completely! Groups of people came out of nowhere, carrying halves of coconuts, going toward the barrel. Aaden saw Shonaia at the edge and asked, "Where can I rest?"

"Wherever you want. We are very grateful," Shonaia replied, dunking her coconut cup into the barrel. Aaden walked into a small hut nearby. There was a straw pallet in the corner. He walked over to it and lay down. He slept for many hours.

In the morning, Aaden slowly crawled out of bed and walked outside. He saw that the hole he had filled with water was surrounded by the village livestock.

"I have to go soon, so I'll just make a lot of water right now," Aaden said to Shonaia, walking to where the water was stored. "*Arogan!*"

It was about three hours later when Aaden had filled all of the barrels. He felt hot and weak, but decided to fill up the watering hole with the rest of his strength before leaving.

"*Arogan! Arogan! Arogan,*" he said, running out of energy. The hole was about halfway full. If he could just manage a few more spells, it would be filled. "Shonaia, get Harlume, my dragon, here," he told Shonaia, just to be on the safe side. After mounting Harlume, Aaden exhaustedly said more spells for water. "*Arogan! Arogan! Arogan. Aro…*"

Aaden's head hurt. It felt like a dark cloud was sweeping over his mind. All the strength left his body. Aaden fell to the ground, eyes just open. Between the slits of his eyelids he saw a yellow light. He slowly opened them about halfway. There was a large shining yellow ball of light in front of him. Inside it was a young woman. Aaden seemed to remember her, but he couldn't quite grasp from where. And then he remembered who it was: the nurse's assistant at the Dragonriders' Academy. She spoke softly to him.

"Aaden, you have overused your powers. Your good deeds were for a good cause, but even good deeds sometimes have consequences. You sacrificed yourself for the village, and for that, I commend you. If I had not come, you would not have survived. I will save you this time, but you will face a penalty. Something very important in your life will be lost. You will not remember this ever happened, and neither will any of the people of the village. Good-bye, Aaden, and let this be a warning to you," she said. Then blackness enshrouded Aaden's mind.

Aaden opened his eyes and felt a pain in his back. He saw Harlume softly nudging him. A crowd had gathered around him. Looking at the sky, Aaden could tell it was nearly night.

"What happened to me?" he asked.

"You blacked out," a villager in the crowd replied. Aaden clambered to his feet and jumped onto Harlume.

"So long, Alpha Capa. I have left much water for you and I must leave," he said as Harlume hovered a few inches above the ground. They headed back to join the others.

"Dive!" Aaden yelled, seeing a small white trail and a few dots in the distance. Harlume plummeted downward. As they approached the ground, Aaden saw a person flapping his arms and realized it was Rederin. Aaden waved and looked at what the group had accomplished. They had made good progress on a shelter in the clearing and started building a track.

"What took you so long?" Rederin asked.

"I, um, fainted, because I used too much magic. What's the giant piece of wood for?" Aaden asked.

"It's the roof. We were waiting for you and Harlume to help lift it. We found lots of rope in the castles," Faten said.

"Where are the knights?" Aaden asked.

"They're over there, working on the track," Cedar said.

"Here, I'll try to lift the roof with magic," Aaden said. He thought about what spell would lift something. "*Mehr don!*" he yelled, staring at the wood. The *X* on his arm went a dull gray. Aaden wondered why that had never happened all the other times he had used magic.

Just as the roof was almost above the walls, Aaden's *X* got duller and duller until the color disappeared completely. The roof slammed onto the walls.

"Knights! Come on! We're going to rest now!" Cedar yelled. In moments, they came darting into the clearing, leading all of the horses and riding their own. Aaden walked into the middle of the clearing, which now looked something like a wooden barn from the outside. Near the middle there were three sacks, one full of gold and jewels, one half-full of nails, and one filled with pots, pans, and utensils. "The door's over there," Cedar said, pointing to a some connected logs that were separate from the walls. There was a small round hole with a stub coming from the bottom on part of it. "We found some blankets in the castles too, and pillows," he continued, walking over to the corner, where a few blankets were. He threw one at each person.

"Let me get Harlume," Aaden said, pushing the door open.

When he got to the dragon, he said, "Come on in, Harlume." *At least the door's huge,* he thought to himself, walking back into the refinery. He laid his blanket down in the middle of the room next to Rederin and crawled under it.

~   ~   ~

"Breakfast is ready! Oh, and Harlume went to hunt, I think," someone yelled. Aaden managed to just open his eyes. He saw one of the knights (not wearing his armor) moving two pans near the group's noses. It smelled delicious and brought Aaden out of his blanket. "Fred and I found some bird eggs about half a mile from here. Darned good luck," the knight said. Now that his armor was off, Aaden realized that the knight was also in his teens.

"Here you go," the knight said, handing Aaden and Cedar a pan with two eggs, sunny side up, a few red berries, and a silver fork. The knight walked over to a smooth rock that they used as a table and picked up two more plates of eggs and berries. Just then, the other knight, Fred, walked through the door, carrying some gold and jewels. He walked into the middle of the room and dropped them onto the short grass. Aaden looked at his timepiece, which read 7:30. As he bit into his breakfast, he asked, "What time did you guys get up?"

"Five or so," Fred replied.

"We're used to it," the other knight elaborated in response to Aaden's gaping stare. He then walked over to Rederin and Faten and handed them a pan.

Rederin and Cedar had gone back to the Forgotten Castles to get more gold. Faten was cutting logs, and Aaden was helping the knights make the track that would go to the Omega Sea. Faten suddenly stopped what he was doing and walked quickly toward Aaden.

"Watch out," he said.

Aaden saw a blue dragon flying toward them. He looked at Harlume and whispered, "Don't attack him yet. Let's see what he's doing. But get ready, just in case he attacks."

The blue dragon landed near them. He walked over to Aaden and stuck out his tongue. On it was a blue stone, which Aaden recognized as the Ruishi Crystal. Next to it was a small, rolled-up note. Aaden carefully took both of them, trying not to get saliva on his hand. Surprisingly, the items were completely dry. He unrolled the note, which read:

Aaden,
I have used the Ruishi Crystal as much as I can.

It has proved very useful in my studies. Please give it back
to Dragondaire. But don't tell them you took it. Oh, and by the way,
that was my dragon, Gard. It doesn't hurt him to keep things in his
mouth,
so don't worry. Give him back the note after you get it.
If you have a quill, write back to me and tell me what you're doing
now.
I'm sure you're working on something big, or else you would have
returned. Remember, the dragonriders are always here for you, and
if you need something, be sure to tell me.
Mr. Ponn

Since he had no quill, Aaden couldn't write a response. He put
the note back into the dragon's mouth, and the dragon flew away
the way he had come. Just then, all seven of the knights came into
the refinery, all without their armor. "The horses are in a small corral,
and so is Harlume," one of them said.

"You guys work fast," Aaden complimented his new friends. He
meant it, too.

"Should we start putting together the stones?" Fred asked.

"Can one of you guys chop wood?" Aaden asked the knights.

"I'll do it," one of the taller ones said.

"The axes are over there," Faten said, pointing to the corner of
the refinery opposite the area where all of the gold and gems were
stored.

"We should probably get four of the knights over to the Omega
Sea to start making boats," Aaden said. "Cedar, do you want to be
in charge of them?"

"Okay, it'll be a break from what I've been doing," Cedar replied.

"You might want to use the horses," Aaden said. Cedar nodded
and walked over to the knights. "I need four of you to help with making the ships," he said.

"Oh, I'm good with making ships. I used to live on Rapid Falls and
had to make a bunch," one of the knights said.

"I'll go," said two other knights in unison.

"Crede, weren't you good with ships too?" the first knight asked.

"Okay, I'll go," Crede said. The four knights walked out of the refinery and picked up their gear. Then they each picked a horse and walked down the track with Cedar. The three other knights walked outside, two of them carrying the sacks of stone and the other carrying an axe. Moments later, Fred came back inside and carried out the other sack of stone. Rederin walked outside to what was left of the pile of wood and began working. The only two left in the refinery were Faten and Aaden.

"Do you want to go look for more eggs to cook for dinner?" Aaden asked.

"Okay," Faten replied.

Chapter 13

Aaden went to the stream, filled his water container, and cleaned the utensils. He gulped down the water and refilled the canister, then he got up and walked deeper into the woods, hoping to find berries or a few squice eggs. Then he remembered that he could make water with magic. Why had he forgotten that? It could have saved a lot of time.

Aaden looked up and saw a thick wooden track. At first he thought it was their track, but then he noticed that the wood looked like mahogany, but he was sure they had used a lighter shade of wood. If this was their track, it was definitely-off course, for if it kept going straight ahead, it would reach Grutch. Somebody must have seen them working and started to make their own! Aaden jumped on Harlume. If he could just get up high, he would be able to look down and have a clear view of all the tracks. "Harlume, fly to where I can see everything!" he yelled as a gust of wind from Harlume's wings whipped his face.

When they were aloft, Aaden looked down. He managed to see two thin lines running through the Northern Woods. One of them ran straight from a brown dot, apparently the refinery, and led toward the Omega Sea. The other began at Grutch and stopped at Drag-ondaire before ending up near Ciliagus. Then he saw a giant army of small dots coming out of Grutch and Dragondaire and heading toward each other. *They must be coming to attack us!*

Aaden had an idea. If he could just get there in time…"Harlume! Go to the Frosty Mountains! Hurry!" he yelled. Harlume shot down in a long dive toward the giant snow-covered mountains far in the west. Aaden looked behind. The sky was a clear blue with white clouds running through it. Then he saw an odd cloud shape, with holes in it. He realized that the cloud was actually a bunch of things with flapping wings. "Dragons! Harlume, *hurry!*" Aaden yelled.

Aaden jumped off Harlume just as he landed and began running through the mountain passes, searching for the place where the four roads met. Then he saw one flat road that went on for quite a while amid all the steep mountains. He remembered running down it with his friends to escape from the armies. He glanced over his shoulder and saw the white things flying closer, but he realized that they were too small to be dragons. "White crows! At least they're better than dragons. But they're still very dangerous," he panted to himself, turning around and running to find the clearing at the intersection of the four roads.

The crows were gaining on Aaden. Aaden saw the clearing just in front of him. With his last amount of energy, he ran into its center and waited. When nothing happened, he jumped up and down, yelling, "Help!" One of the crows sped up and pecked at Aaden's face. Suddenly he felt a jerk as he fell into the ice. *It took them long enough.*

Aaden crashed head first into dirt. "I need to talk to Mr. Ponn, *now!*" he said.

"Follow me," the familiar dwarf said, running down the corridor. "Your dragon will be fine." Memories came flooding into Aaden's mind as he surveyed the walls, doors, and staircases. He almost stopped a few times to look at a picture or statue.

"Here we are," said the dwarf. "He is talking with another student right now, but if it's urgent—" the dwarf was saying, but Aaden swung open the door and ran inside.

"Mr. Ponn! No time to explain! Grutch army! Coming!" he yelled. Mr. Ponn pushed his chair away from the other student, who had a weird expression on his face. He pulled out a drawer and shuffled through paper until he found what he was looking for. He spread out the parchment and scanned it. Aaden looked closer and saw that it was a map.

"Elves! Ready the boys for battle! They don't all need armor. Give dragons to as many as you can! Hurry! And you, Lector, follow the elves!" Mr. Ponn said.

All of the dragonriders were rushed out of the academy and toward the Northern Woods. Those with dragons (including most of the teachers, Aaden, and Mr. Ponn) flew in a group toward the army. Mr. Ponn threw down a rock just as they passed by Ciliagus, and the dragonriders began diving toward the army.

"Fight on your dragons! Swoop as a group! Let your dragons use their talons! Use whatever you have!" Mr. Ponn yelled. At once, all of the dragons' nails stretched out. Aaden couldn't breathe as they were about to make contact. The army put up their shields as the dragons began to attack. Arrows began flying toward the dragon-riders, but they were wearing armor, which protected them from most of the arrows. All of a sudden, a new army appeared from behind the dragonriders. In the back were the other students, some wearing armor. In front of them was the Ciliagus army! Once the Grutch and Dragondaire armies saw them, some of the knights fled. But the brave ones stayed.

Aaden pulled out his sword and swiped off the head of one of the men as Harlume flew near the ground. Just then, Aaden felt a pain in his back. He fell backward and slid off Harlume's tail. His mind went black.

"Aaden! Aaden! Get up, you're in the middle of a war!" Aaden moved his fingers up and down to make sure he could still move. He saw Faten bending over in front of him. Next to Faten was Cedar. Aaden saw hundreds of people fighting each other behind his friends. He jumped up.

"Where's Harlume?" he asked, grabbing his sword from off the ground.

"We don't know. We've been trying to look for him and Rederin—watch out!" Cedar said. Aaden ducked just as an axe was swung above his face. He turned around and swung his sword at a man covered in armor. "*Alama kalaza!*" he yelled. Nothing happened. "*Alama kalaza! Alama kalaza!*" he yelled again, but still nothing happened. He searched the crowd for Mr. Ponn. Far in the distance, a giant yellow cloud was brewing just above the ground. Aaden ran past a few men of the Ciliagus army and got closer to the cloud, which turned into what looked like a giant yellow orb. When he got closer, he saw that the person conjuring it was Mr. Ponn.

"Mr. Ponn, what are you doing?" he asked, ducking to avoid an arrow. Mr. Ponn didn't say anything. Just then, Mr. Ponn shot his hands forward, releasing the orb. It shot through the crowds of men, passing through each of the Dragondaire and Grutch knights, knocking them out. Aaden saw a sword coming at him and blocked it with ease, then he ran over to Mr. Ponn. "What was that?" he asked.

"No time. Navar!" Mr. Ponn yelled. Another small orb appeared in Mr. Ponn's hands and began to grow.

At this point, most of the Dragondaire and Ciliagus armies were fleeing as fast as they could, leaving the Grutch to fight the dragon-riders. It seemed that the dragonriders had the war won, when all of a sudden, red dragons filled the air. Once they were low enough, they began to drop snakes down, and then they flew away. They all ended up in a large mound in front of the dragonriders, but by this time, Mr. Ponn's orb was ready. Just as he had before, he shot forward his hands, releasing the orb toward the snakes. Many of them were killed, but others managed to slide away and start attacking.

"Aah!" someone screamed. Aaden turned around and saw a snake sink its claws into Cedar. Aaden ran over to it and stabbed it with his sword.

"*Alama kalaza!*" Aaden yelled, but still nothing happened. He had a flash of memory, of someone telling him he would lose something. He wasn't sure if it had ever happened or if it was just a dream. Maybe that was what this was about. Had he lost his ability to use magic? Just to be sure, Aaden yelled "*Alama kalaza!*" once more. Aaden felt his *X* go a dull gray color again, and then fade.

"Aaden, Harlume's over there!" Cedar yelled, pointing at a dragon in the sky that was diving toward Aaden.

People lay everywhere. Some Aaden remembered from the Dragonriders' Academy of Learning and Secrets, but others he had never seen before. Aaden, Faten, Cedar, and Harlume searched amongst them for Rederin. Aaden hoped that Rederin had just gotten knocked down or something and was still alive. The Grutch army had mostly died, but some of them had fled back to the city, wrecking both of the train tracks on their way. "How did you guys get here?" Aaden asked, as they sat down and looked out over the carnage.

"Well, I was working on the boats, but I couldn't miss seeing the dust from the whole Ciliagus army, so the knights and I followed them to see what was going on," Cedar replied.

"How did *you* get here?" Faten asked.

"It's a long story," Aaden said.

"We have time," Cedar said.

"Well, it all started when I was looking for eggs for our dinner. I was just walking, and then I saw a strange track. It didn't look like it would lead to the Omega Sea, so I got on Harlume and looked down. But then I saw the Grutch and Dragondaire armies merging together, and they started heading to the Frosty Mountains. Oh, yeah, and there were these white crows that were attacking me. So anyway, I went into the academy and told Mr. Ponn," Aaden said.

"Wait, you went all the way to the Dragonriders' Academy of Learning and Secrets that quickly?" Faten interrupted.

"Yeah, Harlume can fly really fast. So then the dragonriders started fighting the armies, and then the Ciliagus army came, and then I fell off Harlume, and then you guys woke me up," Aaden finished. "Where are the knights?" he asked.

"I don't know. Did you know that you say 'and then' a lot?" Cedar said.

"No, I hadn't noticed. Do I really say it *that* much?" Aaden asked. The group nodded. Faten, who had been walking nearby, fell over and lay motionless on the ground. "What happened?" Cedar asked. He and Aaden crouched over Faten, very worried.

"I don't know, I guess I tripped on something," Faten replied, getting up.

"Hey, isn't that Rederin?" Aaden asked, looking at the body Faten had tripped over.

"Yeah, is he okay?" Faten said.

Cedar bent down and put his hand on Rederin's heart. "He's still breathing. He must have been knocked out," he said. "Do you know a spell to help someone who is hurt?"

"No, but Mr. Ponn probably does," Aaden said. "Mr. Ponn!" Aaden yelled. The dragonrider was across the field, healing the wounded, but he heard Aaden and came over. "Do you know a spell to heal someone?" Aaden asked. Mr. Ponn walked closer to them.

"Spells, spells, spells for healing. A very tricky business, that is. What's wrong with him?" Mr. Ponn said.

"He got knocked out. It's Rederin. We just found him here," Aaden replied.

"That's easy," Mr. Ponn walked over to Rederin. "*Laavery!*" he yelled. A small green orb appeared in his hands. He slowly pushed the orb into Rederin's heart. Moments later, Rederin's eyelids began to open.

"What happened?" he asked.

"We found you here. We won the war," Faten said.

"You okay?" Aaden asked.

"I'm fine; my stomach just stings. I think somebody shot an arrow at me, but it just grazed me," Rederin replied.

Everyone looked relieved.

"So, how did that war start, anyway?" Rederin asked. Cedar and Faten looked at Aaden.

"Well, like I just told Cedar and Faten, I found a strange track. From the air, I saw the Grutch and Dragondaire armies and went to the academy to warn them. Fortunately, we prevailed. But to change the subject, I think the Grutch must have been watching us to see what we were doing with the gold. They figured they could build their own track and take the gold to their country," Aaden said.

"The Dragondaire people fled during all the chaos, and messed up our both tracks in the process, and we don't even know where the knights are," Faten added.

The group realized they needed to get back to their treasures, and they said good-bye to their friends from the academy. They took turns riding Harlume and soon arrived back at their building in the clearing.

Aaden opened the refinery door and looked inside. Two of the knights were in there, eating berries. Cedar walked in. "Where are the rest of you?" he asked.

"No clue. We waited here for you guys to return. Your berries are over there on that rock," one of the knights said, pointing at two plates full of red berries atop a gray rock.

"Oh, and a lot of the track was ruined. Did you know there was another track?" the other knight asked. Aaden nodded and walked over to get his berries. Rederin and Cedar followed. "We did our best to destroy it."

"They're going to be on us like a shot, and once they find the refinery, we're toast," Cedar said.

"If only I could still do spells. I could put an invisibility shield over the refinery so they couldn't see it," Aaden said. Faten looked at him.

"Why can't you?" he asked.

"Oh, I'm not really sure. I just can't," Aaden said. He didn't feel like explaining the weird dream just then. "And besides, I don't know how to make something disappear, especially something as big as a building."

"Could Mr. Ponn do it?" Cedar asked.

"Good idea! I need to hurry up and catch him before he returns to the academy!" Aaden said. "Bye!" He ran out the door and mounted Harlume.

After a short flight on Harlume, Aaden ran over to Mr. Ponn, who was just about to cross the Omega Sea. "Mr. Ponn!" Aaden yelled. The teacher turned around. "Do you know how to make a building invisible, but visible to some people?" he said, panting.

"Why?" Mr. Ponn asked.

"It's a long story, but we're trying to hide a building full of gold from Grutch," Aaden replied.

"I don't know, but I might be able to," Mr. Ponn said.

"Please help us," Aaden said. "Hey, where's your dragon?"

"He's trained to go back to the academy during danger," Mr. Ponn explained.

"Do you mind riding Harlume? One of our knights set Grutch's track on fire and they're probably looking for us. If they find the refinery, they'll figure out how we got the gold. In other words, we should probably hurry!" Aaden said, walking back to Harlume. "You want the front or the back?" he asked.

Along the ride back to the refinery, Aaden told Mr. Ponn about the tracks, the refinery, the plan, and how they had gotten the gold. Mr. Ponn was quite interested, and only stopped him once or twice to ask a question.

"So somebody finally found the famous stream," he said after Aaden had finished.

"We owe it all to luck. I didn't even know what the mist wall would lead to," Aaden said as Harlume beat his wings at an odd angle, beginning a downward dive toward the brown wooden refinery.

Mr. Ponn agreed to try to conceal the refinery from the Grutch. He pulled a brown piece of parchment from his pocket. Aaden watched his eyes scan the manuscript for the right spell.

"Ah! Here it is," he said. "*Invasionkly pearsieblyios, peritebritle, alpheekeyes, cafphraekeese!*" A faint blue light began to cover Mr. Ponn's body, starting at his stomach and extending in both ways. His eyes slowly closed as the blue light began to get thicker and larger. As the light was just about to cover his feet, yellow light shot from him, and there was an extremely loud screech that pierced Aaden's ears. The group closed their eyes and covered their ears, but even so, the screech was louder than anything Aaden had ever heard. It must have even reached Dragondaire!

After the sound faded to a low whisper, yellow light shot up in a wide beam to the sky. Mr. Ponn began muttering a long spell. Aaden could only catch small phrases. "*Alceese...fraer...don-she...claere!*" A green light shot toward the refinery and started covering it like wildfire. Again there was a screech, this time even louder. Aaden fell to the ground with the rest of his friends in response the loud sound and blinding lights. But Mr. Ponn continued muttering a long spell that was never meant to be uncovered.

Aaden woke up the next morning lying facedown on the moss outside the refinery. He got up and looked around. His friends and the knights were still on the ground, in similar positions. Amazingly, Mr. Ponn was still standing, muttering under his breath and staring at the brown piece of parchment. He did not move, and seemed to be in some sort of a trance. Just then, a cool breeze swept through the field. The piece of parchment flew out of Mr. Ponn's grasp. Still he did not move, but continued staring at the space in his hands where the paper had been and muttering. Aaden turned around, but didn't see the refinery. *The spell might have worked, but Mr. Ponn's mad!* He walked closer to the dragonrider and shook his shoulders. Mr. Ponn immediately fell to the ground. Blood streamed down his arm where he had fallen. "*Alphrase!*" Aaden yelled. He had forgotten that he was unable to use magic and was disappointed when nothing happened. He ripped off part of his ragged shirt and put it over the place where the blood was coming from.

Ode to Elves

Elves are
Modest,
Kind and sweet.
Though known
Mostly for their
Pointed ears,
Elves are much more.
Elves are talented
Magicians,
And have unimaginable
Discipline.
They have remarkable
Posture,
Standing straight and tall
At every moment.
Elves are quite amazing, really,
And misunderstood quite often.

Chapter 14

Aaden heard footsteps outside. "Somebody's here," he said. Mr. Ponn stirred.

"You think it's Grutch scouts?" Cedar asked.

"Probably," Aaden said.

"It's a good thing Mr. Ponn made the refinery invisible," Rederin said. Aaden heard someone knock at the door repeatedly.

Mr. Ponn opened his eyes. "Not Grutch. They wouldn't be able to see through the shield," he murmured.

"Then who?" Aaden asked.

"Open the door," Mr. Ponn said, getting up from the ground. Aaden walked across the room and unlocked the door using Rederin's key. Three tall elves stumbled through the door.

"Gatelands," one of them stammered.

"We made it past...gate," one of them panted.

"Who are you?" Mr. Ponn asked suspiciously, now fully standing.

"Fhreeh, Frieke, Fhriler," the third elf said, bending toward the ground.

"Haven't eaten...days," the second elf said in a whisper. Just then, a massive man came through the open door.

"*Procecto diemendo!*" Mr. Ponn yelled. A green light shot out at the man just as he grabbed two of the elves and ran back out the door. The green light shook the wall behind where the man's head had been.

"Fhree! Frieke!" The other elf started to run to the door, but fell a few inches away from it. He got up and ran out the door. There was a loud clashing sound, and then silence. Aaden peeked out the door and saw the large man carrying all three of the elves.

Mr. Ponn ran up to the door and also looked outside. "Navar!" he yelled. Another yellow orb began growing in Mr. Ponn's hands. Cedar, Faten, and Rederin went up to the door and looked outside. The man turned around just as Mr. Ponn shot the orb at him.

One of the elves jumped out of the man's grasp. "*Vbling tee-ages!*" he yelled. A green vortex appeared behind the elf and lifted him into the air. The other two elves floated up with the vortex as the man ducked away from the orb. He pulled out his axe and swung at the vortex as it got higher and higher.

"They're very advanced," Mr. Ponn commented.

Aaden swung his hand in front of Mr. Ponn's stare. "Hello? The man is attacking us!" he yelled. The old dragonrider looked down and saw the man a few feet away, about to slice him in half.

"*Vbling atrium!*" one of the elves yelled. The man froze in his steps and fell to the ground. The elves slowly floated to the ground and walked to the refinery.

The elves were well-fed and hydrated by late morning the next day, and they began to tell their tale. "We were sent from Ciliagus, the most advanced in the army, to pass the Gate," one of the elves said.

"It took us days to climb up the rugged rocks until we passed the Gate. Only barren landscape lay ahead," another elf continued.

"After weeks and weeks of torture, without food or water, we made it to a long brown...corridor. Though the brown walls were only made of air, none of us could penetrate them. The next morning, the brown corridor opened up to a field of green. On top of the tallest hill there sat a giant horse statue that towered into the sky," the first elf said.

"Around the statue were eight giant red orbs, connected with a yellow light running through all of them. Not knowing what to do, we sat down and stared at it for quite some time," the second elf said.

"But then we heard a low growl as the beautiful fields of green turned to beige dirt and sand. Large animals appeared out of nowhere and chased us around the landscape. Just as we were too exhausted to run anymore, we found the corridor and ran into it. The monsters sat at the entrance, growling and gnashing their giant teeth at us," the third elf said.

"We ran for days on end, never going to sleep and never tiring. Then we came to your...building," the first elf said. Aaden was speechless. He'd never heard of anyone making it that far into the Gatelands.

"Wow. I never thought I'd live to see this," Mr. Ponn said. "How did you last that long without food or water?"

"I think hunger and thirst doesn't really exist in the Gatelands. Well, our throats were parched and our stomachs hurt, but we were able to continue traveling," the second elf said.

"Why didn't you turn back?" Faten asked.

"We couldn't find our way back to Ciliagus, and we ended up here," the third elf said.

"So what was the giant statue made of?" Mr. Ponn asked. The three elves looked at each other.

"We've never seen a material like it. It wasn't silver, it wasn't metal, and it certainly wasn't gold," the first elf said.

"What color was it?" Aaden asked.

"Silverish," the third elf said.

"An unknown material located hundreds of leagues deep in the Gatelands. Very interesting," Mr. Ponn said. "Don't tell anyone else about this, though," he warned.

"How did you get so good at magic?" Faten asked.

"Oh, the vortex. Frieke is the one to ask about that," the second elf said.

"Each one of us specialized in one category. Freeh's was internal reading, Fhriler's was sword fighting, and I chose magic. I began training when I was five. I endured many extremes, swimming all the way back and forth through the freezing water of the Omega Sea to the islands, weeks without food or water, and hours under the burning sun of the Halder Desert. I graduated from training when I was thirteen, and I began learning magic. I studied magic constantly for five years until I finished my magic education and was sent off on the mission," Frieke explained.

"Five years…" Mr. Ponn muttered in amazement.

"How did you see through the invisibility shield?" Cedar asked.

"Freeh did it with his internal reading powers," one of the elves said.

"So, which one of you is Frieke, who is Fhriler, and who is Fhreeh?" Aaden asked, confused.

"I'm Frieke," the second elf said.

"I'm Fhriler," the first elf said.

"And I'm Freeh," the third elf said.

"Where are you going to go now?" Faten asked.

"Could we stay with you?" Frieke asked. The Aader and Mr. Ponn looked at each other and smiled.

"Sure," Aaden replied. "We could use some experts."

"Great!" Fhriler exclaimed. "What are you guys doing, anyway?"

Aaden's throat was beginning to hurt from talking so much. "Do you want to tell them?" he whispered to Rederin.

"Sure," Rederin whispered back. "Well where should I start? How about the beginning?" Rederin began.

"We were five friends who snuck away from home to find dragonstones. But first, we needed funds. So we all went to Farmlinder and worked for a farmer named Oodan. Afterward, we went in search of dragons and riches and adventures. But then I was mysteriously poisoned, and they took me to the oracle. Apparently, the rest of the group all went to jail. That's when Aaden discovered magic and escaped. Then everybody except me met up in the Frosty Mountains and were chased by four armies into the Dragonriders' Academy. After a while, they were sent to help the islands. Finally, they had a chance to bring the necessary medicinal plant back to the oracle, and I woke up again. We headed back, but ran into a wall of mist. Once we got through it, we realized we were in the legendary Death Row, and we found the stream and the castles with streets of gold and gems. So then we had the idea to build some type of system to move gold to the islands that need help. We found *graete* to help with that. And then we got involved in a war, and Mr. Ponn came to help protect us from a Grutch attack, and now you're here. And we have a dragon, and a few horses," Rederin finished.

"You went to the Dragonriders' Academy?" Frieke asked.

"Yeah. Mr. Ponn is the headmaster," Aaden said.

"You are?" Freeh asked, looking at Mr. Ponn.

"Yes. My great-great-great-grandfather founded the dragonriders," Mr. Ponn replied.

"Could we join? We've always wanted to be dragonriders!" Frieke asked.

"Certainly. You have amazing talents and you'd make great addition to the academy," Mr. Ponn said.

Betrayal

I will forgive
Or not—
A tough one
After seeing what
He has done.
Betrayal,
The opposite of
Everything good.
But no,
To betray is
Much more than
disappointment
Worthy of tears.

Chapter 15

Flakes of snow were beginning to fall from the sky when the Aader, including three of the knights (who had been wandering around the Northern Woods) and two of the three elves were about to launch the first box along the track, which led to a sturdy ship waiting in the Omega Sea. Rederin carefully opened a lid on the bottom of the box and dumped out a glass vial of *graete* into a steel container. Then he pushed a silver button just above the lid. After a few moments, there was a low rumble from inside the box. Then the box began moving, faster and faster as it moved across the track. "It's working!" Rederin exclaimed.

"How long is it going to take until it gets to Frieke?" Freeh asked.

"Probably a few hours," Rederin replied.

Faten threw a snowball up into the air. "I hope this snow gets harder," he said as the snowball began to fall back down.

Meanwhile, near the Omega Sea, Frieke was staring down the track, searching for the box. He saw it run around a large tree trunk and then continue its path. He turned to watch the knights chopping wood. "*Vbling teeages!*" he yelled. A green vortex appeared behind the elf and he rose up into the air. The knights stopped what they were doing and looked up.

"*Vbling alfradey!*" the elf yelled. Two green strings of the vortex came out from both sides of Frieke and extended over to a thin tree, where they slammed against it. The tree wobbled, then slammed on the ground near one of the knights.

"*Vbling alfradey, sephration!*" Frieke yelled. Five identical strings of the vortex appeared at the edges and began slamming against the tree, chopping it into neat logs. Just then, a large snowball went right through the vortex, causing it to shudder and then disappear. Frieke fell to the ground and looked around.

The large man who had grabbed the elves hours earlier began charging at Frieke. "*Vbling!*" the elf yelled. Another vortex appeared, this time in front of him. The man slammed into it and fell down.

"*Vbling alfradey!*" The vortex shot onto the man, knocking him out completely. The knights were staring at Frieke. Frieke looked back at them, and they pretended like they hadn't been staring, and continued chopping wood. The elf moved his hand forward awkwardly, knocking the strange man into the sea before closing the vortex.

~   ~   ~

Drakint felt something soft fall onto his neck and looked up. He was surprised to see small bits of snow beginning to fall from the sky. His ship creaked and moaned as it slowly moved along the Omega Sea. "Are we close enough?" he yelled.

"No, it is too dangerous, sir," somebody murmured from under the deck.

"Too dangerous? Too dangerous? Nothing is too dangerous!" Drakint boomed back. "Anchor!" A man on deck threw the anchor. The ship started tipping forward from the sudden change of weight. "Pull it back! Pull it back!" Drakint yelled. Three men came from below deck and tried yanking it back, but it was no use. The ship was about to fall over. Drakint ran over to the man and hit him with the flat side of his sword.

"Tidal wave!" somebody yelled. Drakint turned around and saw a giant wave running straight at the tipped ship. With some trouble, he climbed up the ship to where the wooden opening was and dropped inside. He felt the giant wave tear apart the ship and send it into pieces. The area below deck was intact! But Drakint's happiness soon left as gallons of seawater began flowing down. Holding his breath, the teenager struck his sword repeatedly into the wood, eventually making a hole large enough to swim through. He flapped his arms in the water, but the current was too strong and he couldn't move. Just then, he saw a small, yellow, balloon-shaped vessel move toward him. Somebody swam out from the top of the ship and took Drakint inside.

"Drakint, the men are ready. I've designed this underwater ship to fire cannons from below in case any ship tries to intercept your path. Everything will work out just as you have planned, sir," the man said. Just then, the ship bumped into something. "Here we are," the man said, opening a lid at the top of the ship and swimming out. Drakint followed, holding his breath as water flowed in. The man slammed the lid shut, causing small bubbles to appear and float to the surface.

They emerged onto the sand and found there twenty men of all ages, carrying swords, waiting to march into the Gatelands. A scout had listened in on a conversation between three elves, some boys, a man, and some knights talking about a rare material somewhere deep inside the Gatelands. Their plan was to take this substance for themselves, by force, if necessary.

Unfortunately for them, they were noticed immediately by Frieke, who warned the knights to hide out of sight. The knights hid behind trees in a grove as Frieke moved around, getting a closer look at the men. The leader was very short and had golden red hair. "You stay here! I have to go warn the others," Frieke told the knights, swiftly running into the woods along to the track.

"Frieke? Is that you?" Aaden called out when he saw someone running up.

"Yeah. I have very important news!" Frieke called back, running up to Aaden. "An armed band is headed this way. And the leader fits your description of your missing friend."

"Why would Drakint be coming to attack us and take our gold?" Aaden was thoroughly puzzled.

"No idea," Frieke replied. Rederin, Faten, Cedar, and two of the knights had gathered around Aaden and Frieke. Aaden waved at the other knight to come forward.

"We had better get there fast, so we can surprise them," Aaden said, then quickly summoned his dragon. The others mounted horses, and they all sped toward the beach.

Soon all seven knights, the elves, and the four boys were gathered in front of Drakint and the soldiers. "Drakint! What are you doing?" Aaden called from Harlume. Drakint and his men approached them.

"Ah! Former comrades, I am on a quest far beyond the abilities or dreams of you and your little friends. But since you're in my way..." Drakint snapped loudly. All twenty of his men began charging at the group.

"*Vbling teeaganiousae!*" Frieke yelled. A green light circled around the boys and their friends, growing larger each second. Then the light disappeared and a giant cloud of dust appeared, blocking out everyone's vision. But after it cleared, Drakint and his men were nowhere to be seen.

I never thought, of all people—Aaden thought back to when Drakint had taken the coins at Oodan's barn, but he was interrupted by a loud noise. Everyone turned around and saw that the giant box of gold had arrived at the barrier at the end of the track.

"I wonder what Drakint was here for. I thought he was still doing good deeds on the islands. We were heading back to meet up with him," Rederin murmured.

"Was he your *friend?*" Freeh asked. "Well, that spell should have sent them at least fifty miles from here. They might be back, though."

"*Was* being the key word here," Cedar replied, unable to hide the anger in his voice.

"That's that. Let's load up the ship," Aaden said, changing the subject. They couldn't do anything about their former companion at the moment.

"Are you sure *graete* will work on water?" Cedar asked as they all pushed the boat into the water.

"Positive," Rederin said. There was a low rumbling from the Omega Sea. "What the—?" The large ship slowly began to crack near the middle.

"Torpedo!" Freeh yelled.

"*Friehr!*" Frieke yelled. A green light shot into the water. "*Ale!*" The crack started to get smaller. But then there was another low rumble, and the ship shook but didn't crack, and it continued its journey to Alpha Capa.

Something metallic struck Aaden in the back, leaving him yelping in pain. "Aaden!" somebody yelled. Aaden felt blood flow freely out of his body and his eyelids began to close.

Aaden saw a green blur around him. There were dark shadows moving around beside him. Every time they made a full circle, they got closer and closer. Then a giant wolf charged through the green blur and circled around him. "Aah!" he screamed. Then there was darkness once more.

~   ~   ~

He opened his eyelids and saw a dark ceiling above him. He could feel excruciating pain from his wound, and he couldn't move at all. Sweat ran down his face when he made an effort to get up.

"Aaden," something whispered hoarsely. "I have waited years for this moment, training. But now after all my hard work, I find you can't use magic." Aaden heard low laughter somewhere but saw nothing.

"What have you done to my friends?" he yelled.

"Friends? You call them friends? They betrayed you, Aaden. I am your friend now. I am your only friend."

"They would never!" Aaden stammered.

"Hush. You will be able to move later. But for now, you must wait," the voice murmured.

"Get me out of here!" Aaden yelled.

"Why? The world is a dangerous place. You have no friends, Aaden. You have no family. You have nothing!"

"Liar!" Aaden yelled.

"How dare you!" the voice yelled back. Aaden floated into the air and then slammed back onto the ground.

"Where are my friends?"

"Do you not realize? Your friends have left you here. They were to choose one person to go with me. And they chose you."

"You expect me to believe you?" Aaden yelled.

"See for yourself!"

A large misty screen appeared before Aaden's eyes, and he saw his friends around a dark hole, somewhere in the Northern Woods. They carried the unconscious Aaden over to the hole and threw him in, head first. At first Aaden thought it was just a joke...an evil joke. But why was he here, alone and trapped in a dark room? Maybe they really had betrayed him.

"Now, Aaden, think about it. Whom do you believe now, me...or your 'friends'?" the voice boomed. "In a moment, you will be free. Do whatever you like. But don't forget what I said."

Aaden twirled around in circles as the dark room began turning into the light green Northern Woods. All of a sudden, he found himself standing upright. *I'll show them! And all this time I thought they were my friends!* He looked around until he saw a blue area in the distance, probably the Omega Sea, where his "friends" should be. Using all of his strength, he ran as fast as he could toward the sea, next to which he saw a group of people.

As he got closer, he realized that they were his so-called friends But oddly enough, they paid no attention to him. They were all staring at a bleeding mound in the middle of the group. As Aaden got closer, he saw Rederin tying a piece of something around the body, which looked oddly like himself. He ran up to Cedar and reached out to him, but his hand seemed to move right through Cedar, as if it had no substance. Nobody even looked at him. He looked down at the body on the ground and saw that it really was his own body. *Wait a minute. If that's me, then they couldn't have thrown me into that dark hole. They didn't betray me! And that means I'm not Aaden—I'm Aaden's soul! I need to get in my own body!* Aaden awkwardly bent down and lay on his body. He felt a small tingling, and then calmness.

Aaden slowly opened his eyes and looked around. "Aaden, a big piece of metal hit your back, and you seemed to be unconscious," Rederin said.

"Are you all right? That must've hurt," Frieke said.

"I'm fine. I had this really weird *dream*, though," Aaden replied, rubbing his back and getting up. Astonishingly, the bleeding had stopped; he did feel a little stiff and sore. He didn't want to tell them about the dream and how he'd thought they had betrayed him. Looking around, he asked, "Where's the container?"

"We sent it back," Faten said.

"Oh, and somebody needs to fly over to Alpha Capa and tell them about the gold," Cedar said.

"The *graete* container is still almost full. We won't run out for a *long* time," Rederin said.

"Okay, then," Aaden said, clambering onto Harlume, who had grown even larger over the last few days. "Watch for Drakint," he added, floating up into the air.

"Wait a minute! Shouldn't you rest a while and make sure you're okay?" Rederin yelled.

"Really, I'm okay now. Bye!" Aaden yelled back.

Harlume began to dive just as the small ship smashed into the island of Alpha Capa. Villagers gathered around as the dragon softly landed next to it. Aaden slid down Harlume and examined the boat for a place to open it. On the left side, he saw a giant rectangle carved into the wood and pulled on the handle above it. All of a sudden, gold and gems began pouring out from the giant hole.

"What is this?" somebody asked. Aaden turned and saw a man dressed in a leopard-skin robe staring at him.

"My friends and I sent this treasure to help you buy supplies until your village is back on its feet. I can't use magic anymore to get you water, but you can use this to buy what you need," Aaden said, and asked the villagers to help push the boat so that it was facing the way it came.

Then Aaden remembered the key that he had kept in his pocket since the last time he had opened the door of the refinery. Maybe there was a keyhole somewhere. He found a small keyhole on the side of the boat, pulled the key from his pocket, and inserted it. The boat immediately made a rumbling sound and then set out to sea. Aaden said good-bye and hopped on Harlume's back. He was anxious to return to his friends, and hoped nothing bad had happened in his absence.

Chapter 16

Aaden landed near the shore and let Harlume go out hunting while he walked back to the refinery to rejoin his friends. He saw Rederin walking through the trees, and ran to meet him.

"Aaden, we found this piece of paper blowing in from the northeast. Do you think it could be something of Drakint's?" Rederin asked.

"What's it say?" Aaden asked. Rederin handed him the paper. Across the parchment were small lines and circles, divided into groups. He examined the first group of symbols. At the right end was a line going down, identical to the one on the left end of the group. Connecting the two lines was a thin oval, with an X through the middle. "I can't figure it out. Who knows where it could have blown in from?" he said, handing the paper back to Rederin. "Where's the rest of the group?" he asked.

"Uh, they're getting some...stones," Rederin replied.

"Are you okay?" Aaden asked suspiciously. His friend usually spoke in a straightforward way, without awkward pauses.

"Yeah, I'm fine. Just excited about...the...refinery," Rederin said.

"Okay," Aaden said, still wondering what was on his friend's mind. "Did you start making another box?" he asked.

"Yeah. I attached it to the first one. It's loaded and on its way back to the Omega Sea," Rederin replied. Aaden turned around and saw the refinery.

"I thought Mr. Ponn put a spell on the refinery so it would be invisible," he said, looking back at Rederin.

"We're not sure how long the spell will be effective. But I think the stone wall will be strong enough to protect it," Rederin said.

"Have you seen any Grutch around?" Aaden asked. "I'd thought they'd be on to us by now."

"No. It's been quiet, but Freeh said there was going to be a blizzard. I don't know how he knows, but he said it had something to do with the type of clouds and the smell of the wind," Rederin replied.

A gust of wind swept over the handful of red berries Aaden had gathered as they talked, leaving a small trail of them on the ground. "Blizzard," he muttered to himself, putting all of the berries into his cupped shirt and getting up. When they reached the door, he pushed it open with his leg and looked inside. All his friends, including the elves and the knights, were crammed into the middle of the room, surrounding something that was covered by a large piece of cloth. Rederin stepped up to Aaden.

"Aaden Williamson Oaks, we wish to thank you for all you have done for us. Aaden, before you pulled us together and led us on our quest, our lives were going nowhere. We've learned so much, and we've helped others; participated in exciting events, and traveled widely. Let this be a token of our appreciation," he said. Before the astonished Aaden could reply, Cedar and Faten pulled off the cloth, revealing a large statue of Aaden wearing armor and holding out a sword. Under the figure was a flat base, where the words *Aaden Williamson Oaks* were visible. It was a great piece of art.

For a moment, Aaden couldn't say a thing. He was shocked and quite embarrassed. "This is too much, you guys!"

"That's what we were aiming for," Rederin said, smiling.

"How did you make it?" Aaden asked.

"We had a lot of help from Mr. Ponn and his magic before he headed back to the academy," Cedar said. He explained that they had built the statue from an unusual metal they had found in one of the Forgotten Castles. Mr. Ponn had taken a sample back to the academy to find out more about it.

"We're going to put it in front of the refinery," Faten said.

"Oh, so this is what you were trying to hide!" Aaden said to Rederin happily. He would never admit it, but for a minute he had worried that the rest of the crew might desert him like Drakint. But now he laughed at the thought. He needed to stop having such weird dreams.

"You guessed it," Rederin replied, smiling at his friend.

"All right, I hate to break this up, but let's move it, already," Cedar said, and they all helped carry the statue outside.

"This is really incredible of you guys, but you all deserve to be honored as much I do. I couldn't have accomplished anything without your help. I wonder if we'll ever make it into the history books," Aaden said musingly as he helped set the statue down.

"Aaden, where do you want it?" Rederin asked.

"How about right next to the door?" Aaden replied.

The group continued their work. They needed to get the gold to all the islands that needed help as soon as possible, before something else happened to interrupt them. The knights went with another load for Alpha Capa. Freeh, Fhriler, and Rederin monitored the progress of the boxes along the track. Faten, Frieke, and Cedar took the wagon to the Forgotten Castles to get more gold, and Aaden waited at the refinery. If everything went smoothly, they would be finished shortly and return safely to the academy. The boxes full of gold would head out to the needy islanders and come back to be loaded again by Faten, Cedar, and Aaden. While Rederin was waiting, he worked on a new invention, so that when the boxes hit the wooden wall, they would automatically empty.

Aaden climbed a tree to look out for an army sent from Grutch (or anywhere else) to grab the treasure. He was surprised that nobody troublesome had showed up lately, especially Drakint's bunch. The elves weren't sure how far their magic had sent them, but they doubted it was more than fifty miles away. But wait, there it was again: something in the distance, moving swiftly away.

Aaden pulled out his magically enhanced monocular (a gift from grateful Alpha Capa villagers) and looked again. He was pretty sure it was Drakint and his group. Drakint looked very tired and was carrying something small. It was a silvery color, but it had an odd sheen. The group walked toward Grutch, where a large group of small dots was waiting for them. After the two groups met, they headed farther into Grutch. Aaden watched them, wondering what they were up to and what it was that Drakint was holding. Could he have taken something from the Gatelands or from the refinery? Most of the crew had been busy on the coast earlier, and they hadn't thought to leave someone at the refinery. He climbed out of the tree and walked over to join his friends, who had taken a break to eat.

"How's everything going?" he asked.

"Great. I'm pretty sure my new invention will be successful," Rederin replied.

"The boxes are coming!" Freeh said. Everyone turned around. Sure enough, the boxes were coming down the train track.

"Gotta go!" Rederin said, running a few yards in front of the boxes. As they passed, Rederin pushed the red button. All of a sudden, they began to slow.

Aaden told the others about what he had seen, and they all agreed they had better take turns keeping a lookout for trouble. He sent Harlume with a note to Mr. Ponn, asking his help in figuring out the mystery of what Drakint had held in his hand.

The next morning the sun cast golden light across the clearing where Aaden was gathering firewood to use in their cooking fire later. Rederin, Freeh, and Fhriler came running over to Aaden. "Aaden!" Rederin yelled. "Harlume brought a note back from Mr. Ponn. His scouts saw Drakint's bunch going to Grutch, and spied on them. Turns out Drakint stole a piece of your statue. It's been run through many tests, and it turns out it has the power to make whoever uses it much stronger, and also the power to heal most wounds. But it can only be used by one person for a short period of time. The kings of Dragondaire and Grutch heard of this substance and sent men to the Gatelands, but none came back. Drakint's piece is the only one outside the Gatelands, other than the one Mr. Ponn has. He hasn't used it yet, though," Rederin finished.

"Are you sure?" Aaden asked.

"Ask Mr. Ponn—he's coming," Rederin replied. Aaden looked past Rederin and saw the headmaster walking between two trees.

"It might be useful, not for the money, but in case someone is direly hurt. I think I'm going to venture into the Gatelands," Mr. Ponn said.

"But...but...it's so dangerous!" Aaden said.

"They wanted it for the *money* though. They were greedy. *I* on the other hand am going to use it for the benefit of others," Mr. Ponn replied. "So, do any of you want to come?"

"I'll go," a voice sounded. Aaden turned around and saw Frieke looking at Mr. Ponn.

"Okay, I'll go," Aaden said.

"Us too," Faten and Cedar said.

"Does anyone *not* want to go?" Aaden rephrased. No one said anything.

"Well, before we go, we're going to need to pack up plenty of supplies," Mr. Ponn said.

Everyone quickly packed up food and supplies for the trip. They instructed the knights to protect the refinery and be on the lookout for enemies. By the time everything was ready, it had begun to snow once again.

"Let's go!" Mr. Ponn said, taking his first step onto the half-sand, half-dirt of the Gatelands.

Aaden turned around and waved at the knights. "So, Rederin, how's your invention going?" he asked.

"I have everything ready, I just need...something. In case that something is in here, I brought two seprationers," Rederin replied.

"Seprationers?" Faten asked.

"Yeah. I made them myself. They're two little boxes with a wire connecting them on the bottom. If I put one on each side of the right something, it is *supposed* to force things back," Rederin said.

"How did you figure that out?" Cedar asked.

"Oh, some experiments. Actually, it took a while," Rederin said.

The group stopped after walking for hours and built a fire for an evening meal. They had plenty of dried beans and rice from the supplies Mr. Ponn had brought them from the academy.

It was two days later when the group, led by Mr. Ponn, arrived at the legendary Gate, though it looked more like a wall. Huge boulders were piled hundreds of feet high, stretching east and west as far as the eye could see. "I never knew the Gatelands were this big. On maps it looks smaller than the Northern Woods," Aaden commented, gulping some water. "Now, we should probably put our bags up on the smallest rock."

"Do you see one that you can climb?" Mr. Ponn asked.

"Oh, over there!" Faten said, pointing left to where a flat boulder sat; it was about three feet tall. Mr. Ponn climbed up. He had no need to throw his bag up first. The Aader followed.

"Let me see if I can move some rocks," Frieke said. "Uh...*theret controm!*" A small rock about the size of Aaden's thumb wobbled.

"It must be something about this location," Mr. Ponn said, climbing up another rock.

It took hours for the group to reach the top of the Gate; by the time they got there they were tired, bruised, and cold. The snow had picked up, covering the entire Gate with a foot of snow. Aaden pulled out some of his dry fruit and bit into it. It was hard and bitter, but it was better than nothing. Mr. Ponn peeked over the edge of the Gate and looked down. "Uh oh," he said.

"What?" Cedar asked, in between bites of dried apple.

"Blizzard," Mr. Ponn replied.

"Coming from the ground?" Aaden asked.

"Ground blizzard. I've heard of this sort of thing happening here. The weather here doesn't follow the laws of nature. Ground blizzards are much stronger than regular blizzards. They come from other worlds," Mr. Ponn said. Aaden shook his head and crawled to the edge of their rock. Down below, giant snowballs crashed into the Gate.

"What are you talking about?" asked Faten.

"We are but one of several worlds that I have read about. The others are quite different from ours: less advanced, but full of resources that they don't always use. Few know about these lands. I have a book in my private library that describes what we know of them. I suspect that the Gate was meant to separate us from another land," Mr. Ponn said. "But that's just legend. So, anyway, we should try to get some rest, since we can't go down until the blizzard is over."

The group ate some cold food and tried to get some sleep. They could hear the blizzard through most of the night. In the morning they traveled to the bottom of the Gate, and the weather gradually cleared up. As they reached the ground, Rederin slipped and fell headfirst into the snow. They all stopped to eat and take stock of their food supply. Nobody seemed to have much food or water left.

"Well, then, we must be off," Aaden moaned as he pulled himself out of the snow and onto his feet. He was cold, stiff, and hungry. He looked out away from the gate and saw in the distance something that resembled a long brown tunnel about a league ahead. "Look over there," he managed, pointing at the tunnel.

"That's it!" Frieke yelled happily.

"Aren't you tired?" Rederin moaned.

"Not really," Frieke replied.

"Thirsty?" Cedar asked.

"No, but if I was, I would drink. I still have a few bottles of water left," Frieke replied.

"A *few* bottles?" everyone yelled, including Mr. Ponn.

"Yeah, how many do you have?" Frieke asked.

"Only half a bottle!" Aaden said. "How did you manage?"

"I don't drink that much. I told you. I was trained," Frieke said.

"How much *food* do you have?" Faten asked.

"I still have lots of dried meat and apples and oranges," Frieke replied. Aaden almost fainted. When Frieke realized the others were running out of food, he shared his supplies, and everyone had a nice breakfast.

Somewhat revived, the group headed toward the strange tunnel, which, according to Frieke, would be a safe place to walk through. From the outside, it resembled a gigantic worm. Mr. Ponn led them into the tunnel. Inside, away from the snow and wind, the temperature warmed up immediately.

"Warm!" Faten said, falling to the ground of the corridor, which was clean and dry to the touch.

"You okay?" Cedar asked.

"Fine," Faten murmured.

"Frieke, can I have another piece of fruit?" Cedar asked.

"Sure," Frieke said, pulling an apple piece out of his bag. This continued until everyone in the group had taken a piece of fruit. To reassure the others, who were feeling a little wary of traveling in the strange tube, the elves explained that after they walked a couple of miles, the corridor would open up into a large green field. Tentatively, they set out, and gradually relaxed. Sure enough, they soon came to a field of green.

There were many bushes in the field, all seemingly full of ripe and juicy black berries. Atop the highest hill was a giant statue of a horse, miles tall.

"Food!" Faten yelled, running over to one of the bushes and stuffing his face with the berries. Everyone else paused for a moment, then followed him, except for Frieke and Aaden.

"I guess we need to take a piece of that statue back for testing. How do you think we'll manage that?" Frieke asked.

"Go and try," Faten sputtered through purple teeth.

Aaden stood watching the others uneasily. "Guys, aren't you coming? Isn't this what we came for?" he asked. "Mr. Ponn? Rederin?" But they kept eating berries, seemingly oblivious to anything else.

"Who cares?" Rederin said.

"Frieke, you didn't eat any berries, did you?" Aaden asked.

"No, why?" Frieke replied.

"There must be something wrong. I can't get them away from the berries. Maybe there's a spell on the berries," Aaden replied, growing more alarmed as his friends continued their frenzied eating. He walked over to Rederin and tried to pull him away from the berries.

"What are you doing? I'm eating!" Rederin yelled angrily, going back to the bush.

"That's the problem! Frieke! A little help here?" Aaden yelled, pulling Rederin away.

"Stop it!" Rederin yelled, but Frieke came over and together they pushed Rederin away from the bushes.

"Rederin, those berries are bad for you. They're driving you crazy!" Frieke said.

"You're just jealous. You have never tasted delicious food!" Rederin yelled. Aaden was surprised.

"Fine! Go back to your eating," he said, walking down the hill. Frieke followed as Rederin got up and ran back to the bush.

"This place is crazy!" Frieke said.

"I guess we're going to have to leave without them," Aaden said.

"Leave without them?"

"Well, they won't leave on their own. They're just going to have to stay here, if that's how they feel," Aaden said, hurt at his failure to persuade Rederin and wondering what to do.

"Um, Aaden, where is the statue?" Frieke asked.

"Right over—" Aaden stopped in mid-sentence, for after looking up at the hill, he saw that there was nothing there. Just then, a dark cloud began to cover the once-blue sky. In a few moments, small drops of rain started falling.

"Let's get out of here, now!" Aaden said, running back up the hill they had come down. "This place is freaking me out!"

Aaden and Frieke entered the corridor and ran for several minutes before they stopped to rest. "There's something scary about that place. It made the others act so crazy," Aaden said.

"It's a good thing we didn't eat any," Frieke said.

"It's weird," Aaden said. "I'm sure I saw the statue on the hill, and then it was gone. And nobody was there except for us. And nobody could have made a statue that high disappear without anyone noticing."

"Another world...Maybe it was beings from one of those other places Mr. Ponn told us about. Maybe they saw us and made the statue disappear before we could harm it. The other land! They could be powerful enough to make things disappear. They could've easily made it disappear, if they were that powerful!" Frieke said.

"You could be right about that. Maybe that's why people don't return from the Gatelands. They could have put the poison berries there. They don't want us to go into their territory," Aaden said.

"Do you have any food left?" Aaden asked as the sun began to disappear.

"Yeah, I should have some," Frieke replied, swinging his pack around. After looking into the bag, he said, "Hey, this isn't mine; it's Rederin's. I must've taken the wrong one."

"Are you sure it's his?" Aaden asked.

"Yeah, it has that thing inside that he was talking about," Frieke said.

"Wait—weren't you wearing yours the whole time?"

"Hey, you're right. I never took it off," Frieke said.

"That place is getting even weirder," Aaden said, sitting down.

"Maybe some…thing did this on purpose. Hey, wasn't Rederin trying to find out what could make the thing push something the other way?"

"Yeah, so?" Aaden said, not seeing where this was going.

"The statue was made out of the substance he was looking for! Isn't it weird how the statue disappeared and then I found Rederin's thing?"

"You're right!" Aaden said excitedly. "All we have to do is find it," he added glumly.

"Do you think it's somewhere in the other land?" Frieke asked. They reached the end of the tunnel.

"I have a feeling it's not," Aaden replied. "They just want us to think that." Aaden stepped out onto the dirt and sand of the Gatelands. He looked back at Frieke, who was still in the corridor. Snow began to fall.

"Should we head back to the refinery and check on the knights?" Frieke asked.

"Do you want to look for the statue, and try to solve the mystery, and figure out how to save the others?" Aaden said.

"Either way, we're getting out of here for now. And I'm thirsty," Frieke said.

"I'm hungry, thirsty, tired, and sore," Aaden said.

"I know where there's a good clean stream nearby," Frieke said.

"I've probably seen it," Aaden said.

"I doubt it. It's secret," Frieke said, taking another step against the wind.

"Are there animals there too?" Aaden asked.

"Oh, yeah. Plenty. It's their hiding place."

"Do people live there?" Aaden asked.

"None. It's really secret." Frieke led Aaden down a small hole that was hidden from sight by bushes; inside, they went down some rough steps carved into the stone. Near the bottom there was a warm glow, and Aaden could hear the noise of a stream. Frieke reached the bottom first and looked around.

"How do deer get down here?" Aaden asked, stepping onto the dirt of what looked like a large cave.

"That's the question. Nobody knows. And it's a mystery about where all the sunlight comes in," Frieke said, bending down and taking a drink. Aaden also drank before observing the brown animals.

"That's new," Frieke said, seeing a wooden door at the other end of the cave. He walked over to it and pulled. "What the—?" he yelled, slamming the door back. "Let me try that again," the elf said, again pulling the door. This time, Aaden stepped closer to see what Frieke was so excited about. He briefly glimpsed the flickering of many candles before Frieke closed the door again. Then Frieke fell hard on the ground. Aaden tried to catch him, but the elf was too heavy and Aaden ended up falling down too. He wasn't able to rouse Frieke after repeated attempts, so Aaden set about finding food and starting a fire.

A couple of hours later, he had a fire crackling and deer meat cooking, and Frieke began to stir. Aaden had been wondering about what was behind the door, but he was waiting for Frieke, in case it was dangerous.

After opening his eyes, Frieke got up and said, "Come on, let's get out of here." Aaden persuaded him to wait long enough to eat something. After eating, Frieke headed back to the stairway, with Aaden following, very curious and concerned.

"Why the great hurry? What's wrong?" Aaden asked as he climbed.

"Nothing," Frieke said.

"Then why can't we go in? There must be people there," Aaden asked, climbing out of the hole.

"You wouldn't understand," Frieke said.

"Try me," Aaden said. The elf shook his head and started walking at a quick pace toward the refinery, which was still a distance ahead.

"Come on. I won't tell anybody. I won't laugh," Aaden said.

"No, and that's final," Frieke said.

The two of them hurried back to check on the refinery and the knights. Everything was fine, and the knights were doing well at looking after things by themselves, much to their relief. After all the excitement of the last few days, Frieke and Aaden decided to get some rest. Hopefully in the morning they would be able to think of a plan to save their friends. Aaden tried not to worry about what might have happened to them. He would never forgive himself if he didn't find a way to bring them back. He felt responsible for them, and leaving them there was the hardest thing he had ever done. He also tried not to think about Frieke's secret, which was driving him crazy. Frieke probably had a very good reason for not telling him.

"I wonder why the Grutch haven't arrived to attack us yet," he murmured out loud.

"Yeah. We had better scout around tomorrow," Frieke said.

Power

Power:
The entire army
In your hands;
It can be earned by
doing something
Worthy of it.
Power is what
Drives most people;
Everyone wants to have it,
Yet many don't use it
For the good of all.
Power means
Different things
To different people

Chapter 17

"No! You have to send the entire army!" Drakint exploded. His comfortable red chair shook in its place.

The king of Grutch closed his eyes and sighed disapprovingly. "Young Drakint, we cannot afford such a—" he began, but Drakint cut him off.

"You've go to do it!" Drakint yelled, getting out of his seat and walking toward the door. The king shook his head, but began to think about the idea.

A few minutes after Drakint left, the king said to his advisor, "Prepare the entire army to leave immediately, and try to enlist new recruits of all ages from among the townspeople. Oh, and send word to the king of Dragondaire and tell him we need his help to win this." The advisor nodded and strode out the giant doorway. The king walked up the stairs and went to his quarters to get ready. Once dressed, he left his servants to finish the packing and went down to the castle gates. He turned his head when he heard voices.

"Why does the king need to use the villagers too? I mean, how hard could it be to defeat a few boys?" a man said quietly to his son, who was just tall enough to join the army.

"You think it's going to be easy?" the king yelled at the two, startling them. "It *seems* to be easy. But we're dealing with very powerful magic-wielders! We must win so we can take the gold, treasures, and most importantly knowledge that they have!"

And so the king set out with his army.

As the king approached the area where Aaden and his friends had build their rail system, he was surprised to see a dragon sweep across the sky, landing somewhere ahead in the forest. The king could see that two people were riding on the dragon, but he couldn't see who they were. The king raised his scepter high in the air, beckoning the cavalry, who charged forward on their brown horses. Drakint had told him of the building in the woods that Aaden and his friends had made, and that was where he was headed. When they reached it, the soldiers all turned around, waiting for a signal from the king.

"King, the building!" a few people yelled. The king looked up and saw a green half-circle spread from the ground and begin to cover the stone building. When it completely covered the building, it began growing thicker.

At the king's command, hundreds of arrows shot toward the green barrier, and swords were thrust into it. The arrows and swords were thrown back when they hit the barrier, as were any people who were foolish enough to hit it with their bodies.

An elf came out of the building and stared at the king, his green eyes turning yellow. The king backed up slowly, and then turned around and began running to the middle of his army. The elf fell onto his back, and then a boy came out of the building. He knelt down beside the elf as arrows were shot toward him, but none breached the green barrier.

A dragon shot out from the area inside the barrier, and it began shooting fireballs down and dodging small arrows. The king advanced to the front of his army once more. Once close enough, he pulled out an amulet from a pouch hidden under his shirt. He reached forward so that it touched the barrier, which began to crack near the top. The cracks lengthened all the way to the bottom, causing the two halves to fall. The boy managed to get both the elf and himself into the building before the king's army charged in.

Unable to break open the door, the soldiers hacked away until the entire wall collapsed. After the dust settled, the king looked closer, but saw nothing except a sack of gold in the room. Many men ran into the building, unaware of what danger they might encounter.

"Stop!" the king yelled, but it was too late. When the building was crowded with men, a green light replaced the wall that had been knocked down. The king thrust his sword into the light. All of a sudden, he was thrown to the ground, where he lay motionless. The trapped soldiers began trying to push down the new barrier. Suddenly they felt a gust of wind, and the wall disappeared. Many people who were trying to push the wall fell down.

"King, king! Wake up!" cried the soldiers. The king blinked his eyes open. He saw everyone crowded around him and a young boy sitting next to him.

"Where is the amulet?" he yelled. His people looked at him with a weird look on their faces. The king jumped up and walked to where the green wall had been and looked at the ground, but he couldn't find his red amulet. "Find it! And find that boy that was just here," he yelled.

Knights lined up, scanning the ground for the stone, and many of the other soldiers went over to see what was happening. Some of the newer recruits shook their heads and began walking back home, wondering whether the king was crazy to have brought so many soldiers to this place for no reason. Many of the knights joined them, having grown tired of searching for the amulet. Some of them wondered if there really was an amulet or a boy.

Three hundred knights from Grutch were sent out to find the missing boy and the elf, but they all returned with no information. What was worse for the king of Grutch was that his amulet was still missing. The next morning, the king set out alone, saying he was headed for the Frosty Mountains.

"I don't care if it's dangerous!" he yelled before riding off.

Drakint, meanwhile, had been imprisoned for providing false information to the king of Grutch, causing him to send the entire army and many villagers to the refinery for no reason. He was convicted in a court presided over by Chief Rore, a relative of the king. On the day of the sentencing, Drakint sat facing Chief Rore.

"Everyone," Chief Rore began, "we have gathered here today for the sentencing of Drakint, who falsely ordered the army and many villagers to 'war' against, well, absolutely nothing."

"I did not order them, I told the king it might be a good idea!" Drakint yelled, losing his temper. He did this quite often these days. Many people from the audience were amazed at his audacity.

"Well, is the king here? I don't think so," Rore stated calmly. "There is no proof to defend your innocence, Drakint."

"Do you think I *knew* that he was going to disappear right when we got there? I don't think so," Drakint mocked. The chief pounded loudly on a gavel.

"Guilty, guilty," he began. The crowd of people also started chanting. Everyone rose and began walking toward the boy.

"Guards!" Rore yelled. Knights walked over to Drakint and took him by his arms, leading him out of the room. "Dismissed!" As the people in the crowd turned around and began walking back to the front door, Chief Rore walked quickly out of the side door. He went briskly down the stone corridor, looking out through the glass windows at fields of green. At the end of the hall, he began climbing the Rore Stairway, which led to his quarters.

The chief opened his door and looked into his private area. In the northwest corner of the room sat his suit of armor, made from the finest steel and chain mail. Around the armor was his red cape, with its neckline of gold. His dark wooden bed was in the northern corner, next to an enormous window looking down at the Northern Woods. On the eastern side of the room, wooden shelves held swords, shields, and helmets he had collected. He walked over to his armor and began dressing.

After he was completely dressed in armor, Rore put on his cape and went to grab his favorite sword, which he had used to defeat the king in a mini-battle for fun. Next he grabbed his shield and walked out of the room. He closed the door and went down the stairwell.

Fifty men covered with armor and carrying shields and swords were led by Chief Rore toward the Frosty Mountains. Chief Rore was going on a quest to find three sacred objects, which according to legend held great power. The objects—an amulet, a sword, and a scabbard—had belonged to great warriors of ancient times. The objects had absorbed all the power and energy of these legendary warriors. Many had tried to find the three objects. According to the legend, the person who found all three objects would be utterly invincible.

Chapter 18

Aaden found himself standing in a very dark place. He and Frieke had been standing outside the refinery when the king of Grutch noticed his amulet was missing. In the confusion, Frieke had cast a spell to make them disappear. He had no idea where they were.

"Where are we, Frieke?" Aaden murmured.

"Oh, no! Oh, no! *Oh, no!*" Frieke yelled.

"What? And where are the knights?" Aaden asked.

"Here, I'll just tell you everything. Have a seat," Frieke said.

Aaden, very confused, sat down on the slimy ground and tried to make out the elf's body through the darkness.

"Aaden, my name is Frieke Yardes, and I am heir to the Frieke Curse. The eldest male of each generation of my family is named Frieke, and all of them had the Frieke Curse. It gives us bad luck. Where are we? Guess." Aaden had no time to answer before Frieke went on.

"The Frieke Cursed Cave. Sometimes when a Frieke does something that's very important, like the spell I used to get us out of there, they end up in the Frieke Feared Grass. If you go there against your will, you get cursed worse. Horrible, isn't it? Remember that place before, with the stream and the deer? That was the Frieke Feared Grass. You weren't cursed and I wasn't cursed worse, because we went there of our own free will. Past that door is the real cursed area."

"I know what you're thinking: 'Then why were you so freaked out?' This is why. Once in a generation, if a Frieke does something that shouldn't be done, that door appears. When you go in, you're cursed. I'm already cursed, of course. But if I go in that door, I become *really* cursed. Those candles are just a mirage. We're here now, in the cave. Now both of us are never going to be able to leave!" Frieke finished.

Aaden was pretty confused by this account and didn't know how to respond, so he walked around the damp cave, feeling for a door in the darkness. Usually Frieke made a lot of sense, so he tried to give him the benefit of the doubt.

"It's no use," Frieke said.

"Frieke! Look! You're either not as cursed as you think, or you've unjinxed yourself! It's a secret passage!" Aaden yelled excitedly. The elf walked over to him and felt the wall where Aaden's hand was. There was a square piece of wood that fit into the wall.

"Here," Frieke said, pulling on a groove in the wood. A cloud of dust appeared as the square fell off, revealing a small passage just big enough for a small person to crawl through. "You go," Frieke said. Aaden managed to put one of his feet into the hole. From there, he used his arms to hoist his body up.

"Don't come in until I come back, just in case," he muttered before crawling deeper into the passage. As he continued in a straight line, more and more cobwebs blocked his path. Though Aaden was afraid of spiders, he kept going.

It seemed like hours, and thirst was beginning to overcome Aaden, when he finally saw light ahead. He crawled through and found himself in a stone room. Across from him, there was a giant picture of a sword, an amulet, and a sheath. In front of the picture, protruding from a perfectly square rock, was a sword. He walked closer and bent down to where the rock was. On it was carved ancient glyphs that Aaden could not understand. On the third line, in the middle, he saw the word *PUOMES*. As he touched the grip of the sword, a yellow light streamed out from it and shook through Aaden's body like an electric shock. He couldn't move or say anything for moments, then the sword suddenly slid out of the rock. He lay it down on the stone floor and admired its beauty. The long blade shimmered silver, and the hilt was a very dark green, with a hole right in front of where the steel blade connected to the hilt. Aaden grabbed the sword and crawled back to Frieke as quickly as he could.

He dropped down from the hole so he was facing Frieke, who had found a way to light the area with his magic.

"Where did you get that?" Frieke murmured, taking the sword in his hands. As he did, Aaden felt a subtle power deep inside him slowly depart with the sword. "Do you know what this is? Do you even know?" Aaden shook his head. "The Sword of Puomes! Aaden, have you ever heard the famous legend about the sword, the sheath, and the amulet? This is the sword!" Frieke yelled.

"Come on! Are you sure?" Aaden asked doubtfully.

"Aaden, think about this. To get this, you had to end up here, which nobody except me can do, and climb through a long secret passage. Do you think this is a *regular* sword?"

Aaden remembered the carved markings on the wall. *Could it really be?* Aaden grabbed the sword and felt that subtle strength come into him again. He swung it around. Under normal circumstances, since the sword was extremely large for him, he would have dropped it or lost his balance. But oddly enough, he wielded it with unusual grace and agility, turning around and striking into the cave wall. Instead of making a loud sound, the sword went straight into the stone. It then slid right back out, without a scratch.

After Frieke and Aaden had each practiced moves with the sword, a thought occurred to them. "How are we going to get out of here?" Frieke asked.

"Can't you do a spell?" Aaden asked.

"*Vollemar, de...Dragondairian de Vollemar!*" Frieke yelled as Aaden ran his hand down the blade of the sword. Nothing happened. "The sword. If it has the power of the greatest warrior of all time, maybe it can get us out of here," Frieke said, holding part of the hilt. "Now, think about leaving. Let's both visualize being in another place, like high atop a tall mountain."

Both of the them closed their eyes and pictured themselves on a tall mountain. Around them, though they didn't know it, a small, yellow, tornado-like funnel swirled. As they concentrated harder, the funnel swirled straight out of the cave and through its top. They still didn't realize it, but their bodies went through the dirt and rock and into the air. Moments later, the funnel moved west for a while and then dropped. The tornado disappeared, and Frieke and Aaden, carrying the sword, fell to the ground.

Aaden got up and looked around. From where he was, he could see the great cities of Ciliagus, and the blue of the sea beyond.

"Do you think we should go into the Gatelands now?" Frieke asked. "Maybe this sword can take us there too."

"It's worth a try," Aaden replied, getting up. They both closed their eyes and thought about the green fields past the brown corridor in the Gatelands. Again, a yellow tornado spun around them and carried them into the air. After slowly going past a few trees, it began speeding up. In no time at all, Aaden could feel the temperature rise as they rose over the Northern Woods. All of a sudden, they heard shouts from far below. Arrows could be heard swishing into the sky.

"Don't open your eyes," Aaden whispered. The tornado that was holding them slowly began to go downward.

The tornado disappeared, causing the two boys to fall into the grass. Everything was as they remembered it. The grass was just as green, the berries just as black, and the hills as flowery as ever. But Aaden and Frieke were the only ones there.

"Frieke! Get up!" he yelled. There were warriors coming toward them.

Frieke clambered up and looked around. "You use the sword," he muttered, before shouting, "*Vbling teeages!*" A green swirling vortex covered Frieke.

Aaden ran forward, sticking his sword out. When he got closer, he saw that the men were all very fat and much taller than normal.

Aaden swung the sword at the man in front. It pierced through the metal of his armor just as a green ball of light smacked the next man's helmet. The man with the sword sticking through his body pulled it out of Aaden's grasp and swung it backward. The other soldiers pulled out their swords and walked slowly and steadily toward Aaden, their feet all in step. As Aaden bent down to reach his sword, one of the warriors approached him.

"Aah!" Aaden yelled when he felt something hit his head. He fell to the ground. Another warrior swung his sword, but was overcome by a green ball. Just before his eyes closed, Aaden could have sworn he saw Mr. Ponn scurrying around the army.

~   ~   ~

"Aaden! Aaden!" Frieke shook him gently.

Finally Aaden muttered, "Where are the warriors?"

"They're all dead. But I found Freeh, Fhriler, Cedar, Rederin, and Mr. Ponn wandering around nearby. And guess what? There is gigantic city off in the distance. You won't believe it," Frieke said.

Aaden got up and looked around. Everyone was there, staring at him. "What have you been doing all this time? Where's Faten?" he asked.

"Wandering. We couldn't find a way out, and we were really disoriented. We think someone may have taken Faten," Cedar said.

"Wait! Isn't that the Sword of Puomes?" Fhriler said excitedly.

"Oh, yeah," Aaden said, looking at Frieke.

"Well, I don't really want to explain it to you now, but Aaden found a secret passage leading to it," Frieke said.

"But how? Where?" Rederin asked dramatically.

"It was just underground. We happened to be there," Aaden said.

"Should we go look for Faten?" Cedar asked.

"Okay. Do you think he might have been taken to the city?" Aaden said. He turned his head and whispered to Frieke, "Let's not tell them that the sword can take us places just yet. And besides, transporting ourselves in a tornado may not be a good idea here.

A giant stone wall surrounded the enormous city, stretching on and on. The edges were decorated with red designs that seemed to glow. The city seemed to cast an evil dark light around itself, for it was still early in the afternoon, yet the city itself was unusually dark. Giant poles stretched upward from behind the gate, ending in a large cylinder shape, which was slowly moving around and casting a red light downward.

"So how are we going to get in?" Cedar asked. Mr. Ponn pulled his bag around to his stomach and searched around. Moments later, he pulled out a piece of metal shaped like a spider and attached to a very long piece of rope.

"Where did you get that?" Aaden asked, dodging a red light.

"I brought it along, just in case," Mr. Ponn replied. He grabbed the end of the rope with one hand and the piece of metal with the other. He threw the metal toward the top of the wall. Everyone watched as it went just over the wall and fell to the other side. Mr. Ponn pulled as hard as he could. *Clink.* The piece of metal latched onto the top of the opposite side of the gate.

Fhriler was the first to climb up, putting his feet against the wall and grabbing the rope with his hands. Once he was a few feet up, Fhree began climbing, followed by Frieke and Cedar. Once Fhriler was about to reach the top, Rederin followed.

"Agh!" somebody yelled. "Stop!"

"It's Fhriler! Don't move any further!" Aaden yelled, recognizing the voice. There was a clash of metal and then another scream, but this time a low-pitched scream. It was followed by panting, and then silence.

"You can come now," Fhriler muttered from the top of the gate. The chain of people continued moving, led by Fhree, who was about to climb to the top. Mr. Ponn was the last to climb up the gate, pulling up his rope.

"This place is huge!" Freeh said. Aaden walked over to the edge, amazed. For what seemed like miles on end, there were giant stone buildings sticking high up into the air. It was like a giant version of Ciliagus, just not as happy-looking, because of the darker light cast on it. Near the middle was a giant building, which looked like a castle. It was surrounded by a large gate about the same size as the gate leading into the city. Giant men, some ten or eleven feet tall, covered in gleaming silver armor, were slowly walking around the buildings.

"So the choices are: jump down and try to escape the knights; jump down and try to fight the knights; climb down, risking that they might see us and shoot arrows or use magic before we get to the bottom; or use magic and try to kill them from here, also risking that they'll kill us with arrows and magic," Aaden said.

The group agreed to try magic first. "*Vbling teeages!*" Frieke yelled. But this time, nothing happened.

"Maybe magic doesn't work here," Freeh said. After several more tries from Mr. Ponn, Frieke, and Cedar, the Aader thought of another plan. Fhriler, who was a champion sword-fighter, would first jump down and kill as many of the warriors as he could. According to Frieke, it would be easy for the elf to handle them all in combat.

"Are you ready?" Frieke asked.

"As ready as I'll ever be," Fhriler said. Pulling out his sword, he let his legs fall over the edge. "Five, four, three..." he murmured. When he reached zero, he pushed his body forward and began a long fall. Halfway to the ground, many of the warriors began lugging their huge bodies toward the gate. Fhriler landed on his feet.

"Nice landing," Freeh commented. Everyone watched as one of the warriors towered over Fhriler and swung his giant sword down. Fhriler was ready, though, and jumped to one side. Luckily, the warrior was still bending down, and the elf swung his own sword into the armor. The warrior looked up and swung his sword toward the top of

Fhriler's head. The elf pulled out his sword and blocked the attack just in time.

After defeating two of the warriors, Fhriler put down his sword and picked up one of theirs. After swinging it a few times, he walked toward another knight, who was walking at an extremely slow pace toward him. He swung the giant sword at him, which pierced through the metal armor. The knight's body shook and he swung his sword down. Fhriler was cut on the side of his neck when he tried to duck. In anger, Fhriler grabbed his adopted sword and pulled it out.

"Agh!" the warrior yelled. The elf threw the sword toward the knight's head and ran away. Moments later, the blade spun around in circles and knocked off the warrior's steel helmet. Fhriler bent down and picked up his own sword. He ran forward and performed a series of deadly sword moves, going from low to high and high to low, causing the nine-foot-high monster to fall down.

Since the rest of the warriors were still behind, Fhriler took a moment and bent down near the warrior's head. It was all brown and very small. The chin was pointed, and there were two equally pointy ears on top. It was completely bald, and its yellow eyes shone eerily. Fhriler got back up and turned around. He saw Aaden putting one of his feet down on the stone ground.

"Are you tired?" Aaden asked.

"A little," Fhriler replied, handing Aaden one of the warriors' swords. "Same person?" he asked. Aaden nodded and walked toward one of the knights.

Everything seemed to freeze as the two boys speedily circled the knight and stabbed him.

"I see you've entertained yourselves, boys," a voice said.

Aaden stopped in mid-step and looked around. He saw a man of normal height standing in front of him. He was wearing a piece of carved, shiny rock on his head and was wearing a large black robe. Behind him on both sides were two more warriors. They were even taller than the other ones, more than twice the size of the man and a little less than three times the size of Aaden.

"Welcome to Temeye, man of the other land. I see you've had a lot of fun with my WarPice," the man said. Frieke stopped fighting and looked at the man.

"Where are we?" Aaden demanded.

"Temeye—I just said that," the man said. All of a sudden, there was a series of noises, and then the tapping of feet. Aaden turned around and saw the Aader running toward him. "Oh, you've brought more. More fun," the man said. "Follow me. And don't try to stray," he added, snapping his fingers. A few warriors crowded around the group, led by the man and the two bigger knights.

"My name is King Temeye, leader of the Temeye forces. And you?" the man asked, beginning a quick walk toward the large building near the center of the city.

"Why do you need to know?" Mr. Ponn asked.

"Excuse me?" the man asked angrily.

"Where are you taking us?" Fhriler asked, still holding out his sword.

The king turned around for the first time and looked at the elf. "You think you can beat me, King Temeye, founder of the Temeye forces? You, a puny little elf with only that small sword of yours?" he asked, stopping.

"Answer my question," Fhriler said, holding his sword higher. The king pulled out his own sword and swung it toward Fhriler's, which was knocked away. Frieke and Aaden gasped in surprise. The man put his sword back into its sheath and continued walking.

"I am taking you to the Temeye castle, where you will have a chance to win your freedom," he said. All of a sudden, Aaden ran between two of the warriors and picked up a giant sword. King Temeye looked at him queerly and snapped his fingers. One of the giant warriors at his side walked toward Aaden. He swung his sword down, but Aaden parried the attack, causing him to lose his balance and fall down.

Just then, thousands of arrows began pouring down from the tops of high buildings. "*Run!*" Aaden yelled, dropping his sword. The Aader began running in every direction, trying to dodge the attacks. Aaden heard a sound from behind and turned around. Frieke was lying on the ground with six arrows in his back. He ran over to the elf and carefully pulled out the arrows. "You okay?" he whispered, pretending he had also been shot.

"Don't know," Frieke murmured. Aaden felt rough hands raise him high. He looked down and saw that one of the giant warriors was holding him about fifteen feet up in the air. Next to him was another warrior, identical to Aaden's, holding up Frieke. He looked down, but was not cheered when he saw Freeh, Fhriler, Cedar, and Mr. Ponn lying in a heap. Smaller guards were walking to them.

Creativity

In case by chance
You find yourself
In a sticky
Situation,
Creativity can prove
Much more useful than
Force.
Creativity:
The things that
Come straight from your
Imagination,
Without passing through
Rigid rules.
Knowledge:
The things you learn in
School shouldn't always be
Valued over
Creativity.

Chapter 19

Aaden opened his eyes and looked around. He was in a stone cell with no windows, and there were several bars blocking the entrance. He was lying on the ground, and he felt very sore near the small of his back.

"Aaden, are you in there?" someone asked.

"Uh huh," he replied, still not able to move.

"It's me, Frieke. Cedar, you, and I are in a line. I don't know where everyone else is."

"Where are we?" Aaden asked.

"We're in the giant building in the center of Temeye," a new voice said, which Aaden recognized as Cedar. "Do you hear that?"

"Hear what?" Frieke and Aaden asked at the same time.

"Listen." They heard a *tip tap, tip tap.*

"Hi," said Rederin to Aaden.

"Rederin?" Aaden asked, surprised.

"What's happening?" Cedar asked.

"It's Rederin," Aaden said.

"How did you get out?" Frieke asked.

"Let me get you out first," Rederin said, staring into Aaden's cell. Rederin found a pair of keys on a ledge near the other side of the wall and unlocked Aaden's cell quickly.

"How did you get out?" Aaden asked as Rederin walked to Cedar's cell on their right.

"I didn't get in. They didn't catch me. I snuck in here in between two of the warriors, and they didn't notice me, so I looked for you.

And you know, this prison is huge!" Rederin replied, twisting the key. Cedar walked out and stood next to Aaden.

After unlocking Frieke, the group walked down a corridor, looking in each cell.

"Help me," one man groaned. Aaden looked into his cell. He was an old man and his white hair was becoming very bushy.

"If we have the chance, we'll come," Aaden said, feeling very sorry for the man. He wanted to help, but he was afraid he might get caught, which would lead to more trouble.

"Aaden!" somebody called. Everyone turned around and saw Faten standing behind bars. "Thank goodness you came!"

"Shh," Rederin said as he unlocked the door. Faten ran outside. The group continued walking quietly, taking a right turn, then another right turn, and then a left.

"Look," Aaden said, pointing into a cell where Fhree and Fhriler were sitting. They were both lying on their sides, apparently sleeping.

"Not yet. Keep them here for a while," Aaden heard someone mutter. Everybody froze in place and made no sound.

Frieke was the first to slowly turn his head. "Rederin, you unlock them," he said. Rederin rushed to the bars and stuck in the key.

"Come on, guys," Aaden whispered into the cell, shaking Freeh. Finally, Freeh's eyes opened, and he nudged Fhriler. They both got up immediately and walked out of the cell.

"They're coming," Frieke said. Everyone ran down the long corridor and took the left turn nearest to them.

"They're not here!" someone yelled. Everyone ran faster down the hall toward a door at the end.

"We don't have the sword," Fhriler muttered as he pulled the handle.

"We'll find it later," Aaden said, rushing in.

Inside the dark room, lit only by four flickering candles, was a large bookshelf on one wall. *Creak.* All of a sudden, the shelf began to turn around, revealing Mr. Ponn, who was hanging from his wrists at the top. "Mr. Ponn! What happened?" Aaden asked, running to him.

"Don't know," Mr. Ponn said. "Try the keys," he added, shaking his hands. Rederin came over and jumped up, sticking the key into a hole. After jumping two more times, he managed to turn the handle, causing Mr. Ponn to drop to the ground.

"What if they get into the red tower?" somebody outside the room yelled.

"Don't worry, sir; it's guarded very well. And they wouldn't think to look under the carpet. And they don't even know the password to get up the stairs," said another voice.

"You'd better be right. You'd better be right," the first voice said. Then there was some murmuring, which nobody could understand. Next there was complete silence, and no footsteps could be heard.

"Come on. Let's go," Freeh whispered, walking to the door.

After following Rederin through several more turns, the group found themselves at a corner. They stopped there because many loud noises could be heard, noises that sounded like metal against metal. "I'll check," Fhriler said, peeking over the edge. "It's more knights—hundreds of them, guarding a giant stone door," he said, pulling his head back.

"*Hundreds?*" Aaden asked.

"Shh. They're going to hear you," Rederin said.

"Okay, maybe not *hundreds,* but lots," Fhriler replied. "And nobody has swords."

"*Look!*" Mr. Ponn yelled. Everyone whipped their heads around and saw Temeye and about forty warriors chasing them.

The group was too shocked to move. "Go past them," Aaden whispered. "*Now!*"

Everyone was scratched by the warriors' armor as they attempted to run on either side of the giant group. Luckily, the knights were obviously not very bright, and it took King Temeye quite some time to herd them all the other way.

"Go up the stairs!" Freeh yelled.

"The knights will have problems, since there are so many!" Mr. Ponn yelled, pointing at a red staircase a few yards away.

"Password?" a deep voice yelled as they approached it. All of a sudden the stairs were covered by a giant piece of wood.

"King Temeye is the greatest king!" Aaden shouted. The wood moved suddenly, revealing the staircase once more. "What the—?" Aaden yelled, running up.

"How'd you know that?" Rederin asked, running by his side.

"I guessed," Aaden admitted, peeking over his shoulder. The knights were closing in on them, but as the first few began going up the steps, most of them tripped, causing others behind them to fall.

"Get up there after them!" Temeye yelled.

Rederin and Aaden were the first to get to the top of the stairs "On the count of three, run past those two guards," Aaden said, pointing to a dark red door lined with gold, which was guarded by two small warriors. Rederin nodded. As the rest of the group took their last steps on the staircase, Aaden said, "One, two, *three!*"

The guards turned their heads and pointed their swords, trying to get to the door as the Aader raced forward. Mr. Ponn ran swiftly toward the door and threw it open. Aaden and Frieke were next, both ducking and sliding into the opening.

Faten was the last person in, and he tried to close the door. Everyone joined in the effort, for Temeye's group was now smashing into the door. One of the warriors managed to stick his sword through the door, just missing Mr. Ponn's head. More swords followed, making holes everywhere.

"It's too dangerous standing here!" Aaden yelled.

"Look—the window!" Frieke yelled, running to the opposite wall. "It's either that or wait for them to come in!" he yelled, pulling the window open. The rest of the friends quickly joined him. The door began to creak, and then it fell inward. Immediately, guards started piling into the room.

"Jump out the window!" Aaden yelled, and then he jumped head first out of the window.

Everything was a blur as he plummeted toward the ground. For a moment, it seemed to Aaden that he was dreaming, and that if he could just open his eyes and awaken, he would be home, safe with his family in Dragondaire, away from all these warriors and knights. But that wasn't the case, and he knew it, so as he fell, he covered his head. All of a sudden, he felt himself bounce on something soft. Opening his eyes, he saw Frieke standing in front of him.

"Are you okay?" he asked.

"Fine," Aaden replied. Just then, there was a big jolt as Fhriler and Freeh landed next to them on the hay.

"Thanks for moving the hay there," Freeh said, opening his eyes.

"No problem, but where are the rest?" Frieke said. Everyone exchanged glances, but no one spoke.

"Hey, where are we anyway?" Aaden asked, looking around. Behind him was the wall of the tower they had just come from, and in front of him was another wall.

"Well, I think this is the place we saw in the middle of Temeye," Rederin said.

"There has to be a door leading back in," Aaden said.

"Back in?" everyone said, staring at Aaden.

"Well, don't you want to save the others? And they stole the Sword of Puomes. We can't just let them keep it!" Aaden said.

"He does have a point there," Frieke said.

The group crept around the corner of the wall and peeked around the edge. Not seeing anybody, they continued, then halted abruptly.

"That's going to be a problem," Freeh said.

It was a large entrance, and there were many giant guards marching in front of the giant stone door, swords in hand. And to make matters worse, there was another heavily guarded gate nearby, leading into the city.

"Wait! Do you hear that?" Aaden asked. Faintly, he could hear what sounded like horses' hooves stomping on the ground, and it was getting louder. Then there was a loud moaning sound as a few of the guards hauled open the door leading into the city.

"It's a carriage. Guys! We can jump onto it and pretend we're with them!" Freeh said rather loudly as more guards hauled open the other door.

"Here it comes!" Aaden said excitedly. A few horses appeared through the open gate and trotted slowly toward the door leading into the castle.

"Follow my lead!" Fhriler said. He walked forward just as the brown carriage drew near.

"Ow!" he said, pretending to fall down. He quickly got back up and jumped onto the carriage. At first Aaden didn't think it was going to work, but nobody seemed to notice that the elf *hadn't* fallen off of the carriage. But then again, the giants *were* a little on the dim side, and everyone on the wagon looked asleep. Aaden and Freeh ran up to the wagon and climbed onto it at the same time.

"Move aside, now! People are coming through!" Aaden yelled. He almost laughed at himself afterward. Frieke also jumped onto the wagon.

"Watch out, people!" he yelled as the wagon entered the stone building. All of a sudden, it came to a sudden stop, and the three boys jumped off. They ran to the back of the wagon and bent down. Through the cracks in the giant wheel, they saw a man dressed in a blue robe walk out, followed by two normal-sized knights covered in steel. The men walked to the end of the corridor and took the stairs up. After they were out of sight, Aaden got up and looked around. To his right were two doors, one of which was lined with gold and had a keyhole near the middle.

"Let's go in that door," he said pointing to other door. "It might be the armory, or something else useful."

The door creaked open slowly as Freeh pushed it in, revealing a darkened room full of cobwebs. Near the middle was a box, and beyond that was another door. Fhriler walked forward and grabbed the box. He pulled the top off, causing little bugs to fall out.

"Ew!" Fhriler said, dropping the box. There was a clink as it hit the ground upside down. Curious, Aaden turned it over with his shoe. Inside, among the spiders and beetles, was a key.

"This could be useful," Frieke said, picking it up. He dusted it off and wiped it on his shirt.

"Hey, it might unlock that other door, the gold one," Aaden said.

"It's worth a try," Frieke said, walking outside. He stuck it into the hole and turned it right, then left. All of a sudden, the door swung open. They went swiftly inside. There, lying on a table, was the Sword of Puomes.

"There has to be some catch," Aaden said walking slowly toward the table. Just then, a series of things happened very quickly. First a rope came up from the ground and wrapped itself tightly around Aaden's feet, causing him to fall to the ground. Next, a giant net came down from the ceiling around Aaden. Then many red lights shot down from the ceiling, anchoring the net and trapping Aaden. And to make matters worse, a loud alarm went off.

Within moments, footsteps could be heard outside. The elves jumped behind four barrels lined up in the corner of the room, being careful to avoid the red lights around Aaden.

"Hey, what's this?" Freeh whispered, turning around. Frieke looked over his shoulder and could make out a small square door at the bottom of the wall.

"It's a trapdoor. But let's not go in it yet. We need to save Aaden," Frieke said, turning his head back. In between the cracks of the giant barrels, he saw Aaden frantically struggling to free his feet. A dark-hooded figure entered the room, pressing a red button on the wall and causing the alarm to stop. His black hood swayed as he came closer to the still-struggling Aaden. He stretched his arms so that his bony hands protruded from his sleeves. In his right hand, a white ball appeared and began to grow. In his left hand, another ball appeared, but as this one grew it got redder and redder.

When it touched the red lasers surrounding Aaden, his body glowed eerily, but after passing the light, he stopped glowing. By now, Aaden had backed off as far as he could.

"Aaden, Aaden," the dark figure breathed. "I never doubted you would make it here, but what a pity. You, a legendary boy who could be heir to the Four Kingdoms, trapped—and what's more, you're unarmed!"

"Who are you? Are you even human?" Aaden asked calmly. "And how do you know me?"

"To some extent, I am human, but to you I am a ghoul. And everyone of this world knows you," the voice whispered.

"How?" Aaden asked.

"We have visited your world many times before and watched you and your friends. Why have you not seen us, you wonder? Because you aren't as advanced as the people of Temeye. But now I really must destroy you!" the ghoul said.

Both of the glowing balls rose up about a foot and stopped growing. The red one quickly turned into fire and shot toward Aaden. Aaden tried to escape it, but it was too large, and it whipped past his face. He was terrified beyond screaming, and his face was slammed against the stone ground. Then the white ball shot at Aaden, but stopped about a foot away from him and spread around the net, becoming rock-hard ice. Then it spread closer and closer to Aaden, eventually freezing him in place.

Frieke was the first to jump out, running closer to punch the ghoul's face. Instead of making contact, his fist went right through the ghoul's head, which turned very light, almost transparent. All of a sudden, another layer of ice quickly spread around the elf, trapping him just like Aaden. Freeh jumped up, knocking down a barrel, and ran up to the ghoul. At the same time, Fhriler ran toward the table and grabbed the Sword of Puomes, just as the ghoul sent another layer of ice over Freeh. When the ghoul saw that the elf had the sword, he screeched loudly, piercing the air.

Fhriler was about to stick the sword into the ghoul's body when a blurry form flew into the room, picked up the ghoul, and flew back out the door in the blink of an eye. The elf was stunned at first, but after the shock was over, he laid the sword on the ice covering Frieke. The ice began to soften, then started disappearing from the top down. Next Fhriler went to Freeh, and then Aaden. The three brothers were able to free Aaden from his bonds with the sword. At first they all just stood there, dazed and shivering. A few minutes later, they started to feel better.

"What was that?" Freeh said.

"He said he was a ghoul. And did you see that bird fly into the room?" Aaden said.

"Yeah. It was weird, and really fast," Frieke said.

"At least we have the sword back now," Fhriler said. They all walked out of the room.

"You think the others are still in the room in the tower?" Freeh asked, looking around furtively in the direction of the staircase they had taken earlier.

"They've probably been captured by now, but it's worth a try," Aaden said, and they started walking briskly.

They quickly reached the staircase and the tower, and Aaden slowly pushed open the door, which was now full of holes from their earlier adventure. To his surprise, there were many people in the room, including King Temeye, Rederin, Faten, Cedar, and Mr. Ponn, but none of them were moving. The warriors' swords were pointed toward their friends. Fhriler, who was still holding the sword, walked past large groups of knights over to Mr. Ponn and patted him on the shoulder. At first, nothing seemed to happen, but then Mr. Ponn started to glow a red color and started blinking.

"What happened?" he asked.

"It's a long story, but let's free the others and get out of here before we talk," Frieke said. Fhriler walked through warriors to reach Cedar, Faten, and Rederin. They were able to free them the same way Fhriler had done. Afterward, they grabbed swords from the frozen warriors and walked out of the room and down the staircase.

"How are we going to get out now, even with swords?" Faten asked. "We're no match for the hundreds of knights guarding the inside door and the outside gate."

Just then, there was a loud screeching noise and another one of those weird blurs passed them and headed down the hall. Aaden felt a weird feeling that started in his feet and quickly ran up to his head. He was frozen in place and couldn't move at all. He tried to blink, but nothing happened. In front of him he could only see a blur, like the outline of a dark figure and a sword. Then he felt himself lift a few feet into the air and glide back down the hall toward a brown blur.

Aaden didn't remember anything after that. Eventually he awakened from his dream state to find himself stuck to the floor in a completely dark room. He had no idea where he was. He realized that someone was speaking to him, or near him, anyway, in a soft resonant voice, a voice that sounded powerful and authoritative. He couldn't quite make out what the voice was saying, only small parts of it.

"You...Puomes...amulet...sheath...statue, here...wish you luck," the voice said. Then there was a loud windy noise, gusts of air, the creaking of a window, and then nothing. Aaden felt pain in his right arm, as if someone had punched him. He tried to speak, but nothing came out. Then there was a much greater pain, and he could tell somebody had just stepped onto his stomach. He started gasping for air, and finally the man moved away. Aaden felt another pain as plates of metal scratched against his side. He knew he must be bleeding, for the crack between two plates had pinched his skin.

He heard the sound of a creaking door. Aaden was now bruised and bleeding, but he still couldn't move, and he couldn't see anything around him.

Chapter 20

There was sunshine and bright colors all around. There were doors and beds and food and water. Everything seemed so happy and calm, but then a blur flew in, breaking windows and turning everything black. Swords, arrows, and axes started appearing, flying around and breaking things. Warriors began piling into the room, and then a new group arrived. The two groups fought, and people started turning gray. Then everything turned dark and nothing could be seen. Next, there were prison cells blocked by stone walls, filled with dirty men grabbing onto the bars. Another blur flew into the room, stopping and laughing at the prisoners one by one, making fun of them. There were more and more prison cells, with more and more prisoners, with more laughing blurs speeding around laughing at the prisoners.

"Aaden, come on! Wake up!" Aaden felt himself being shaken. He tried to shake the dream out of his mind. He was lying on the stone of a large street. On both sides of him were great stone buildings in rows. In front of him were Rederin, Cedar, Faten, Fhriler, Freeh, Frieke, and Mr. Ponn.

"What happened?" Aaden asked.

"You won't believe it!" Rederin exclaimed.

"Really, you won't," Frieke said.

"You see, we were all frozen, and then this great big bird picked us up and carried us out here," Rederin said.

"A dragon? Here?" Aaden questioned.

"It wasn't a dragon," Fhriler said.

"It was smaller, had pointed wings, and was encased in a big purple bubble," Cedar said.

"You were shivering really badly," Faten said.

"The guards didn't notice?" Aaden said, sticking to the subject.

"They froze when it passed them," Frieke said. Aaden got up and looked around. Just in front of him was a crossroads.

"Okay, shouldn't we get going? Now that we have the Sword of Puomes, we can protect ourselves from Grutch!" Faten said.

"The sword!" Fhriler exclaimed. "Where'd it go?"

"It's gone *again*?" Aaden asked miserably.

"Well, if all of the guards are frozen, it won't be too hard getting in," Mr. Ponn said, walking to the intersection. Aaden followed with the rest of the Aader, thinking hard.

From the outside, the castle looked like a giant box near the ground, with several round towers sticking out of it.

Thinking of the sword, something occurred to Aaden. "Hey, you know how there's supposedly a sheath and an amulet to go with the sword, and how people have searched for them for centuries with no luck?" Aaden asked. "Well, the sheath and the amulet could be in one of the other worlds, like Temeye."

"Good point," Mr. Ponn commented. "They could be anywhere. It would be easier to search if I could call my dragon to come and fly us around. I've been working on a way to call my dragon," Mr. Ponn said. "*Dragihn, dragihn,* you are here, you are here. *Vreeh-lange, vreeh-lange kraw!*" he yelled. Everyone covered their ears.

There was a creaking sound, and a window from a very high tower popped open, revealing the hooded head of another ghoul. The friends crammed themselves against the wall, afraid to make a sound. Then there was another creak, and the window slammed shut.

A few minutes later, Aaden heard a steady flapping sound. The group had been waiting patiently to see if Mr. Ponn's dragon would respond to the call. Suddenly something green and dragon-like flew over them. Just then, there was a big booming sound. Aaden turned around and looked up at the castle. At the top of one of the towers, two giant wooden doors had opened up. Going in and out of them were several red and blue birds surrounded by purple mist. When the mist touched the dragon, it froze in midair.

"I didn't think of that," Mr. Ponn said apprehensively, watching the birds fly away from his dragon.

"Well, we could get the sword first and then think of a plan to free the dragon," Aaden said, feeling the wooden door.

Suddenly the sky turned very dark, startling everyone.

"Wow, that was cool!" Faten said.

"Let's go find a place where we can hide and sleep," Frieke said. "We can't see in this light, and we all need rest."

After an hour, the group found a good place to sleep near the front gates of Temeye, where there was a grassy area with trees and bushes so they wouldn't be visible. The ground was soft, and though they had no bedding, most of them were sound asleep within a few minutes. Aaden and Frieke were both awake for a while, worrying about what might happen if somebody evil got hold of the sword, the amulet, and the sheath.

Everyone woke with a jolt to a horribly loud noise the next morning.

"What in the world?" Mr. Ponn yelled. Everyone jumped up, feeling stiff and sore, and looked around. There it was again—another loud noise, but this time Aaden thought he recognized the sound. It sounded like a wild dragon's fire slamming against something.

"Dragonstones!" he and Rederin said together.

"There are dragons here?" Cedar asked.

"Let's go see!" Freeh said excitedly, sprinting down the street.

Near the castle, the group looked up into the sky and saw something quite extraordinary. Many feet above, they saw four blurry bird-like creatures about half the size of dragons, three blue and one red. The blue ones had a grayish mist around them and the red ones had a purple mist. They were slowly circling around a wide area. Around them were six flying ghouls who were shooting fire and ice at them. When the ice hit the mist, it seemed to stick there, growing. Once it had grown fairly large, it shot to the bird next to it, which sent it to the red bird without letting it even touch its mist. In front of that bird it stopped, double in size, and started sizzling with fire. Then it shot around at an incredible speed, circling the inside of the circle of birds. The ghouls all shot fire above the middle of the bird circle, where it connected, separated, and then shot toward the birds. The animals let the fire go into their mists. Moments later, they all shot out fire to other birds. When the fire came to their mists, it increased speed and shot around.

Just as the group watching thought they couldn't possibly be any more confused, a giant bird (similar to the smaller ones fighting, but as big as three adult dragons) flew out from behind the castle and circled above the smaller birds, leaving a hurricane of fire starting only a few feet above the others, who had stopped moving from fear. Once the giant monster got to where it was only a speck atop a fire hurricane, it traced the fire path back down again, but not touching the fire. It left a trail of ice, which joined with the fire to form a blue liquid. The liquid shot in ten beams toward the ghouls and small birds. The ghouls, taken by surprise, were pushed to the ground. The small birds sent fire into the middle of their circle, which rose above the giant bird. Next, the fire circled above all of the dragons, evaporating most of the blue liquid. The rest of it, though, joined back together and returned to the giant bird.

All of a sudden, four blue glass containers rose from the ground and trapped the birds. Then, a giant green missile rose up next to the base of the glass, causing Aaden and Faten to jump aside.

Aaden felt something wrap around his stomach, and looked down. A rope was tightly wound around his stomach. Then he felt himself being pulled swiftly backward, his stomach full of pain. He looked to his side and saw his friends also being pulled backward.

"Aah!" everyone yelled.

Just then, Aaden screamed as his back slammed against a stone wall. Then his pain stopped, his eyes closed, and he dropped to the ground and blacked out.

Some time later, Aaden opened his eyes and tried to move, but found it was very painful. His back was still hurt. He looked up and saw King Temeye standing over him.

"I now have the Sword of Puomes, and there's nothing you or your friends can do to stop me from taking over your own world!" he yelled.

Aaden tried to move, but he was still bound by rope.

"Give me the sword," a voice said simply, which Aaden recognized as Mr. Ponn's.

"Excuse me?" Temeye asked.

"You heard me. Give me the sword," Mr. Ponn said. After waiting for a response, the dragonrider did a flip and ended up standing on his feet in front of Temeye. The guard aimed his sword at him, but was too slow. Mr. Ponn jumped around the guard and kicked King Temeye. Temeye turned around, and to everyone's surprise, he ran back toward the wall. The guard slowly lugged his body in the same direction to protect his king, but by this time Frieke, Freeh, and Fhriler were already up. Frieke and Freeh ran up and punched the king in his stomach and jumped into the air, dodging the warrior's attack. Amazingly, Frieke didn't fall back down until he was many feet above the knight's head. Once they were next to each other, the elf locked his hands around the knight's neck and wrapped his legs around his body. Fhriler ran up and punched Temeye with all of his strength, causing him to fall to the ground. Meanwhile, Freeh was untying the rest of the group.

"Score!" Frieke yelled. There was a loud, metallic *clank* as the guard fell to the ground. As Freeh untied Aaden (who was last in line), Mr. Ponn and Freeh looked for a door leading out. Frieke and Fhriler made their final jumps onto the huge guard. Nobody noticed at first that King Temeye had walked out the door.

"King Temeye!" Faten yelled, but the king had already exited the room.

"Let's go!" Cedar said, pulling open a door.

"What about Aaden? His back is still hurt," Rederin pointed out.

"You go. I'll just wait here," Aaden said.

"Are you sure? You might be captured," Mr. Ponn asked.

"We'll all be captured if you wait for me," Aaden said.

Aaden, left in the dark alone and in pain, was worried. He figured he had broken his back since he still couldn't move.

Minutes seemed like hours as Aaden lay there trapped in a dark room without anyone else. He grew extremely bored as the hours passed and the room grew darker. *Have they forgotten about me?* Crazy ideas filled his brain, and he couldn't concentrate on anything important. He was afraid to sleep, for fear that he might be captured, and he was really uncomfortable.

Chapter 21

"Aaden! Great news!" someone yelled. Aaden slowly opened his eyes. He didn't know how long he had been sleeping. Near the now-open door, standing there with his arms full of bags, was Rederin. Once he moved into the room, the rest of the Aader followed in, each carrying more bags.

"We found the kitchen, and there was a ton of food!" Faten said excitedly, bending down next to Aaden.

"Are you okay?" he asked. Aaden shook his head slowly.

"What took you so long?" he gasped.

"We got the sword!" Frieke said, holding the Sword of Puomes in front of Aaden's face.

"We had to battle six ghouls and we got frozen twice, but it was worth it to get the sword back and this much food," Freeh said. Cedar nodded in agreement.

Mr. Ponn closed the door; there was just a dim light from a window on the east wall. "We're going to have to stay here for a while, until Aaden feels better," he said.

Rederin held a drumstick above Aaden's face and asked, "Aren't you hungry?"

In response, Aaden opened his mouth, bit a large piece of meat from the bone, and chewed slowly. After he'd eaten and Mr. Ponn had rubbed some ointment on his back, Aaden began to feel a lot better, though his back was still stiff and sore.

"What next?" Faten said.

"How about we look for the sheath and the amulet before we leave this world?" Frieke suggested.

"How are we supposed to get up there?" Cedar asked.

"I have a plan, but I'm not sure if it's going to work," Aaden said. "Follow me."

Aaden led the group to the red staircase, and a guard's voice boomed, "Password!" Fhriler handed Aaden the Sword of Puomes.

"I have the Sword of Puomes. If you do not answer my question, I will kill you with it," he said.

"What is your question?" a deep voice said calmly.

"Where does this castle keep the birds?" Aaden asked.

"You mean the swithers?" the guard asked.

"I don't care what they are!" Aaden yelled, trying to sound menacing.

"Okay, okay! Go down to the staircase at the end of the corridor," the guard said, pointing a finger. "You'll see three doors. Use this key to open the door right in front of the staircase," the guard said, throwing a metal key over the wall. Mr. Ponn caught it and handed it to Aaden.

"Thanks—I mean, okay," Aaden said, remembering to sound mean. The soldiers in this world certainly were cowardly, slow, and stupid. "Let's go," he said, walking down the corridor left of the staircase.

Aaden stuck the key into the hole in the door and twisted it to the right. Pulling the handle, he twisted the key to the left. The door swung open, revealing several blurs flying around in a dark room. Immediately, several of them began flying toward the open door. Aaden slammed the door shut, breathing hard.

This time Aaden was ready. With the Sword of Puomes at hand and with Rederin sticking the key into the hole, he pulled open the door. When all of the birds were flying toward him, he stuck the sword in front of them. A few of the birds in front lost their mists and retreated to the back of the room, where they were only dim lights in a sea of darkness. Still keeping the sword out, Aaden got rid of the rest of the birds' mists.

"How'd you know they were going to do that?" Frieke asked.

"I guessed," Aaden said, walking into the room. He walked in front of one of the smaller birds that was resting on the ground, and looked it over. Its face had pointy feathers sticking out that looked kind of sharp. Its beak was exactly like a triangle split in half by a line. It had two wings with more pointy feathers, and its tail looked like a smaller wing, but very long. All in all, it looked like a very poor drawing of a dragon, except for its tail, which reminded him more of a snake with feathers. Aaden carefully put his leg around the bird's body, behind its right wing. He adjusted himself, and pretended he was sitting on Harlume. To his surprise, the bird didn't even quiver or try to shake him off.

"First we'll unfreeze your dragon, Mr. Ponn, and then we can go look for the sheath. We can travel on these...swithers," he said.

After everyone had gotten onto their own bird, Aaden touched the Sword of Puomes to all of the beasts, revealing their mists. He had hoped this would happen.

"Left?" Aaden said.

"Just tell me where to go," came a voice. Aaden almost fell off.

"Did you just say something?" he asked.

"I'm not that stupid. Well, where do you want to go?" the bird replied.

"Wow, I wish dragons could talk," Aaden said. "Can you take us out of the castle?"

Immediately, Aaden's bird pushed off with its feet and beat its wings. Following Aaden's, all of the other birds also lifted into the air and flew out of the room.

"Can you talk too?" Faten asked his bird as they flew down the corridor. His bird sadly shook its head.

The birds led the Aader to a very high tower, where they flew out an open window. Aaden looked down once they were high above the castle and was amazed to see the Temeye River behind the castle. It stretched on, continuing to circle for miles and miles.

"Wow!" he said.

"Where now?" his bird said, beating its wings up and down so that it hovered in place. Aaden looked around, searching for a dragon. Spotting a green shape near the castle, he stretched his hand down so that it was in front of his bird's face, and pointed to the dragon. In a few moments, the bird began speeding toward it.

Aaden turned around, seeing the others on their birds behind him.

"This is weird!" Faten yelled over the roaring wind. Aaden nodded and turned his head back. All of a sudden, the bird he was riding began a steep dive toward the green shape about fifty yards down.

Near the dragon, all of the birds stopped. Aaden, balancing carefully, slowly stretched out the Sword of Puomes and carefully nudged the dragon. Like they had planned, all of the birds except for the one Mr. Ponn was riding on flew away from the dragon as it frantically beat its wings to stay airborne. Mr. Ponn's bird slowly glided to the dragon. Once they were about to touch, Aaden's bird glided over to Mr. Ponn's, and Aaden passed him the sword. Mr. Ponn touched the sword to the bird's mist, which slowly disappeared. His bird went forward a few inches so it was touching the dragon, allowing Mr. Ponn to carefully climb on.

Now that Mr. Ponn was on his own dragon, the bird he had ridden just moments before was free. But instead of flying back to the castle, it stayed next to the dragon as it joined the group.

All of the birds flew in a circular formation past the Temeye castle, so they could explore and look for the sheath and amulet. The area behind the castle looked very much like the area they had already seen, with many large buildings arranged in the same manner. There were no clouds, and there was only a dim light.

"What in the world?" Mr. Ponn yelled.

About a mile in front of the group were several pointed shapes, hovering in a circle.

"Go to that circle," Aaden said to his bird.

As they got closer, the Aader could see that the hovering figures were all sheaths. But once the group was within a few yards, the sheaths moved out of their places and started chasing after the Aader.

"Go to the middle!" Aaden yelled, for within the chaos, he could see a sheath in the middle of where the sheaths had been, but it wasn't moving. "To the sheath that's not moving!" he added, dodging a sheath.

As they got closer, the object looked less like a sheath and more like a green tube. But as soon as Aaden approached it, all of the sheaths left what they were doing and returned to their original circle.

"Aaden!" someone yelled.

Aaden whipped his head around and saw a sword flying in the air toward him. He knew that if he didn't catch it, they would never make it back out of this world. He reached for it and missed. He looked down and saw the Sword of Puomes plummeting down.

"Go!" Aaden yelled. The bird he was riding on was already beginning a steep dive. Even when it passed the falling sword, it continued to dive straight down. Aaden couldn't believe it. In this respect, a swither had a lot more control than a dragon. Aaden's bird leveled near one of the castle towers, directly under the sword.

"Look out!" someone yelled from above. Many birds with mists were flying out of an opening at the top of the tower opposite. As Aaden paused to look, he missed the sword. His bird, however, managed to catch it in his mouth.

Aaden and his friends quickly returned to the sheaths, which were even harder to get past than before. The rest of the group tried to distract the sheaths, and, finally, Aaden and his bird made it into the circle.

Like before, as he approached the tube, the sheaths rushed back in, blocking the other birds, who were trying to get into the circle from above and below. Aaden grabbed the sword and touched its tip to the tube. At first it just shook, but moments later, it began to stretch and expand, until finally a boy popped out of the top and slowly floated onto Aaden's bird. Aaden, very surprised, exclaimed, "Did you just pop out of that tube?"

"Um, um...uh huh," the boy said in a low voice. "My name is Nesohc Namuh Semoup Eutats," he said, then floated back up into the air toward the tube.

"Wait!" Aaden called, but it was no use. The boy had already disappeared into the tube, which was now shaking uncontrollably.

"Aaden, let's go!" Rederin yelled. Aaden, disappointed, dived down on his bird with the rest of the Aader.

That night, they slept again in their hiding place, lying under Mr. Ponn's dragon's wing for warmth. They had decided to let the birds go.

Most of the group thought it would be best to leave Temeye in the morning. Frieke, on the other hand, was thinking about something else. He was thinking about Aaden's encounter with Nesohc, not a disappointment, but a true discovery. As everyone else lay sound asleep, he lay down, moving his finger along the ground.

It was early the next morning when Aaden was nudged in the shoulder by what felt like a sharp beak. Opening his eyes, he looked around.

To his surprise, one of the birds was standing in front of him. Then he saw other birds hitting his friends with their beaks.

"Come on, let's go. I want to see *your* world," the bird said in a high-pitched voice.

Aaden looked around. He saw the others starting to get up. Mr. Ponn's dragon was sitting peacefully a few yards away. *We might as well travel in style,* he thought.

Once everyone was on a bird (or a dragon, in the case of Mr. Ponn), they set out on what would turn out to be a very memorable journey. Aaden would carry the Sword of Puomes, and Mr. Ponn, who was good with directions, would lead the way.

But first, the group needed food. They had pretty much finished with the food they had pilfered from the castle. Rather than break into the castle again, they thought about knocking on the door of a smaller building to see if they could purchase a meal. They decided to knock on a door and see what happened. It was Rederin's idea, so he knocked on the door of a house on the outskirts of town. It was a three-story stone house, and the door was engraved with silver. Mr. Ponn figured the richer the house, the more generous they might be.

Rap tap tap. Rederin's knuckles hit the big door three times. There were several rustling noises, and then a cracking sound. A small rectangle suddenly opened near the top of the door, too high for them to see into.

"What do you want?" came a voice from inside. It sounded like a woman, and she was either very annoyed or just angry.

"We are a group of travelers who are in need of food!" Mr. Ponn boomed loudly, surprising everybody.

"Oh. Well, then, leave your weapons and your birds outside," the voice said. Aaden, suspicious, put the Sword of Puomes down loudly, and then very carefully picked it back up and put it behind his back. In a moment, the door carefully opened. From the inside, the house looked rather like the dormitory of a boarding school. There was a magnificent rectangular table covered with goblets and plates. Against the walls were wooden bureaus. In front of them was the woman who had just been talking to them. She was wearing tailored black and white clothes, lending her the appearance of a servant.

"Why don't you have a rest while I prepare breakfast?" the maid asked.

"That would be great," Mr. Ponn said.

"Right this way," the servant said, leading the Aader around to a door on the right. She opened it to reveal another magnificent room. There were six neat beds along the north and east walls, and there were fluffy blankets and pillows on each one. The sheets were pure white, and everyone felt like jumping onto them. Covering the entire floor was a bright red carpet with golden squares and lines and all kinds of images on it. Along the west wall was a brownish couch, covered in wrinkles. In between two beds on the east wall was another door that had impressive carvings of flowers and land-scapes. Doors like that took many months to carve. They were very rare in Dragondaire and Grutch.

"Well, then, why don't you have a rest? Make yourselves at home, and don't worry about messing things up. I'll go make you some breakfast," the lady said, leaving the room.

To be polite, they all just sat down on the couch and waited. They studied the excellent furnishings, tapestries, and ornaments.

About twenty minutes later, breakfast was served. Everyone was seated at the table under an elaborate light fixture. The food looked delicious. Each diner had two gold-and-white eggs, three pieces of something brownish, and in the center of the plate was a golden sphere. Next to the plate was a gold-rimmed goblet, and two forks and one knife atop a folded white piece of cloth.

Everyone was curious about the golden sphere in the center of each plate. It looked and felt like the inside of an egg, except it was filled with a thick brown liquid that tasted like melted chocolate. Everyone tried to savor these and make the delicious substance last as long as possible. Mr. Ponn was the only one who didn't eat his.

The woman stood by the left door throughout the entire meal, staring at them, and especially at Aaden. But once she saw that everyone was finishing, she came in and started clearing the table. It was then, as Aaden stood up, that he realized he didn't have the sword.

"I don't have the sword!" he whispered.

"What?" several of his friends said, trying not to be too loud.

"Did you have it when we were waiting?" Rederin asked.

"I had it in my lap. I didn't put it anywhere," Aaden said, worried. "She must have taken it somehow."

"But we would've noticed," Faten said.

"Well, there's only one way to find out," Mr. Ponn said. He got up from his chair and slowly opened the door.

Inside was the woman, who stood there staring at him.

"Yes?" she asked, a nervous look crossing her face.

"Have you...did you take the sword Aaden was carrying?" he said sternly.

Just then, there was a noise, and a boy walked up, carrying the Sword of Puomes.

Everyone, even the elves, knew it was Drakint.

"Drakint!" everyone exclaimed—that is, everyone except for Mr. Ponn.

"You guys are *so* last year!" Drakint yelled. "Did you think people in Temeye would just let you into their houses and give you food like that? Hah!"

"Give the sword back," Aaden said calmly, causing everyone to turn their heads away from Drakint and to look at him.

"Ah, if it isn't Mr. Know-it-all. Aaden, isn't that your name?" Drakint said. "Well, who really cares? Who really cares? Oh, you want the sword? Why don't we play a game first? You like games, right?" Before Aaden could say anything, Drakint continued. "Okay, I'm thinking of a number that's between one and...a trillion. You get three guesses."

"Nine hundred ninety-nine million, nine hundred ninety-nine thousand, nine hundred and nine!" Freeh said dramatically.

"Lucky guess," Drakint sputtered. "I'll give you the sword if you guess right two more times." There was a pause, and then Drakint said he had another number in his head.

"No, you won't," Freeh said simply. Aaden slapped his hand against his forehead, remembering the elf's powers.

"Yes, I will!" Drakint yelled.

"I don't think so," Freeh argued.

"How do you know that?" Drakint yelled again, beginning to lose his temper.

"It's kind of obvious, you know," Freeh said, realizing his mistake.

"Okay, I have another number," Drakint said.

"One trillion is not a number *between* one and one trillion," Freeh said, forgetting his intention not to argue.

"Ugh!" Drakint yelled. "But you still don't get the sword!" All of a sudden, the boy ran past them toward the door leading outside. Since the group had been taken by surprise, Drakint was already outside by the time they reacted. They chased after him, running past Mr. Ponn's dragon toward the gate.

"So long!" Drakint yelled. All of a sudden, a dragon swooped down from over the gate and scooped him up.

"Get on my dragon!" Mr. Ponn yelled. They realized that their swithers had disappeared, and they had no time to find them. Everyone looked for them, but it was no use. Drakint was probably at full speed heading toward Grutch, where he was apparently very welcome.

"We can't all fit on your dragon," Aaden pointed out.

"It's our only hope," Mr. Ponn said, jumping onto the front of his dragon.

They all climbed on, and the dragon awkwardly made to take off. Once the dragon was in the air, Frieke said, "Once we get out of the Gatelands, I can make a vortex and take a couple people off so we can fly faster. Watch carefully, in case we catch a glimpse of Drakint."

"Where are we going, anyway?" Faten asked. Mr. Ponn looked back at Aaden.

"I guess we can head to the refinery and regroup. Grutch and Dragondaire will probably find out that we found the Sword of Puomes, so they'll probably try to hunt us down," Aaden said.

Chapter 22

They had only been riding on the dragon for a short while when they saw flying shapes in the distance, steadily getting closer. Aaden's heart sank, and he got a horrible feeling in his stomach. He thought this was going to be the end. The shapes looked very menacing, like some sort of evil creatures riding large birds or small dragons. And Frieke still couldn't use his magic.

"Get out of the Gatelands before they get to us!" somebody yelled from behind.

"Our only hope is magic! We have no weapons, and my dragon is going to be slow, since he's carrying so much weight!" Mr. Ponn yelled over the roaring winds. The sleek, dark shapes now surrounded them. The faces of the riders were hidden behind dark hoods, and only their bony fingers were visible, sticking out of their cloaks.

"Dive!" Mr. Ponn yelled down.

His dragon, very well-trained, plummeted downward. But as he increased speed, so did their pursuers, who must be ghouls, though they remained above them. The ghouls got into a circular formation, and half of them shot fire into the center of their circle. The other half shot white balls into the same place. Then the fire and the white balls collided about ten feet above Mr. Ponn's dragon and raced toward the dragon, forming the shape of a curved blue shield which quickly swung in front of the group on Mr. Ponn's dragon. The dragon couldn't stop *that* quickly, and he slammed into it, causing the shield to thicken.

The shield continued to grow, surrounding them. When there was just a few inches between them and the wall, Frieke yelled, "*Amare partiones tiones!*" The blue wall exploded into small shards resembling glass, and fell in all directions toward the ground.

"Keep going just a few feet," Mr. Ponn commanded his dragon. "Then stay."

By the time the ghouls had realized what had happened and got over the shock of their shield having broken, they kicked their legs up into the air and shot toward Aaden and his friends. But they were much too late. Frieke had already sent green bolts at them, knocking a couple of them toward the sea, causing the other ghouls to regroup. With the extra time, Frieke created another green vortex next to the dragon. He, the other two elves, and Aaden jumped on.

"Go to safety!" Aaden yelled to the group. "We'll take care of it!" Once he saw the concerned look on his friends' faces, he added, "We've got it. No problem."

Before leaving, Mr. Ponn made his mark by sending four bright yellow orbs toward the ghouls.

It seemed like it was all going to be okay, and that they could defeat the ghouls. There were only three ghouls left, and Frieke had already sent one green bolt toward them. It was then that they noticed a great number of ghouls rising from the water. Ghouls obviously didn't die. They were quickly recovering their strength and joining the others.

"Oh, great!" Freeh sighed.

"How are we supposed to kill them?" Fhriler asked.

"We can't worry about that now. We need to get away and chase Drakint for the sword. It's the only way," Aaden said.

"Hold on tight—we're going to *varp*," Frieke said. "*Varpelar!*" he yelled.

The flat vortex they were standing on turned into a thin strip that was holding up the elves and Aaden. Suddenly, they were secured in place by magic, and couldn't move their feet. Then a green wall came up. It bent and slowly fitted itself with amazing precision around everyone, faces and all. At first everyone was scared, Frieke included, but then they realized they could breathe and that they were now moving away from their pursuers at an incredible speed.

Aaden tried to turn around, but couldn't. From the sounds behind them, he could tell that the ghouls were chasing after them.

"*Speedeir leir!*" Frieke managed to yell.

All of a sudden the boys stopped moving. But a split-second later, they found they were moving again. They were actually moving so fast that it was hard to tell whether they were moving or not.

"*Freeh go!*" Frieke yelled, his eyes still closed. A few moments later, the strip the boys were standing on turned a sharp left.

Aaden felt like he was going to faint or throw up. Nothing he had ever experienced had prepared him for this. But as he tried to open his eyes once more, he felt something push against him.

"*Freeh!*" someone shouted. Then there was another turn, another left turn.

"*Speeder leirdno!*" Frieke yelled, and the strip slowed.

There were several sighs of relief when they opened their eyes. Aaden looked to his right. He saw Mr. Ponn, Cedar, Faten, and Rederin standing next to him.

"When did you get here?" he asked.

"No clue. One minute we were sitting in the refinery, and the next we were flying at full speed on this…thing," Cedar said.

Frieke, meanwhile, looked back behind the wall. Seeing the ghouls some distance away, he said, "If we continue at this speed, we'll have just enough time to get to Dragondaire."

"Why are we going to Dragondaire?" Cedar asked. "And why don't we get rid of them?"

"Drakint's probably either there or in Grutch, and we're not ready to go into Grutch yet. And those things from Temeye don't die," Frieke said.

"*Guys!*" somebody yelled. But it was too late. Something had made the transportation device Frieke had created disappear, leaving everyone to plummet toward the tops of trees. They found that they couldn't move, and they had no idea who had done this to them.

Aaden opened his eyes. He saw a red orb enclosing everyone. Since it was partially clear, he could look outside. He saw hundreds, maybe even thousands of floating blurs. He tried to say something, but nothing came out. To make matters worse, he couldn't move, either. Since he had been falling before he got frozen, he was in a very uncomfortable position.

"Aaden, why…why…no, what are you trying to do, for pity's sake! What are you trying to accomplish?" a voice said. "Oh. Fine, I'll let you talk."

Aaden felt like he could move his mouth, so he tried to ask who was speaking to him, but he didn't think anything came out.

"Oh, you think you're in charge, huh? Do you think I'm really going to reveal my identity to you while you're frozen in a Draenon-aball?" the voice hollered.

"*Darder wan,*" Aaden whispered. It was the only spell he could think of at the moment, curse or not. He had forgotten that his magic powers had been taken away, and he was just a little bit surprised when nothing happened.

"Good one! Good one. But no, all magic is blocked while you're in this Draenonaball," the voice said. "Man, I've always wanted to have you in my control. So, what to do now? What to do now? What do I want from—what in the—" The voice came to a sudden stop. Through the red wall, Aaden could see several blurs fly toward the bubble. When it looked like they were about to reach it, he felt a shaking and the ball disappeared.

Aaden closed his eyes as he fell toward the ground. He was used to this by now, and he wasn't that scared. Suddenly he felt himself land on something hard. He was still in the air, though. He looked around and realized he was lying across Harlume. Quickly sitting up, he was even more surprised to see eight more blue dragons, each carrying one of his friends. And there was one more, a larger one, leading the group of dragons around a man floating next to them, obviously entrapped by some spell. But wait—he wasn't riding Harlume! The dragon he was riding was too small. Harlume was the dragon riding in front.

"Aaden, Harlume had babies!" someone yelled.

At first Aaden couldn't believe it. It was too weird. Harlume was male. Well, how did he know that he was male? He had just assumed it. Well, he had obviously been mistaken.

"How do you know they're his—uh, hers, I mean?" he called back.

"They look like him, I mean her, and I've never seen this many dragons in the same place before!" Mr. Ponn called.

"I can't believe it!" Aaden yelled, still trying to take it all in.

"What are you going to name them?" Rederin yelled. But before Aaden could answer, someone yelled, "*Fring!*" It sounded like Frieke, and Aaden noticed the floating man was now encased in a green ball floating in midair.

"Who is that, anyway?" Aaden asked. Even though it wasn't a command, all of the dragons circled around the green barrier Frieke had made. Inside, without a doubt, was Drakint, frozen and holding the Sword of Puomes. He obviously hadn't recognized Drakint's voice earlier because of distortion caused by the spell.

"How does he do that?" Faten said.

"Do what?" Cedar asked.

"Just appear every single place we go!" Faten replied.

"Should I let him talk?" Frieke asked.

"I'd like some answers," Aaden said in response. Frieke closed his eyes. Moments later, a very tiny voice from inside said, "Let me out, let me out!"

"It's funny when he sounds like that," Rederin said. Aaden had to agree.

"So, Drakint, what have you been doing lately?" Aaden asked.

"None of your business," the tiny voice called back. Before saying anything else, Aaden couldn't help but laugh.

"How about this deal? We'll let you out...but you have to answer all of the questions we ask you and give us the sword," he said.

"No, thank you!" Drakint tried to yell.

All of a sudden, Aaden was somehow thrown from his dragon.

"Hah!" he heard Drakint call. But almost as soon as he had begun falling, he felt himself being picked up again by a different dragon. As it flew up into the sky, he looked up. He saw all the dragons frantically trying to escape balls of fire that were being thrown at them.

"Harlume!" Aaden yelled. "Tell the dragons to put us all down on the ground, then get them to break the barrier. Then get the sword from Drakint and bring it down to us!" he finished. He sure hoped Harlume was listening.

Sure enough, Harlume made an odd roaring sound. Immediately, all of the small dragons dove toward the ground and into a small clearing.

Setting everyone down, the dragons flew back into the air, where they joined Harlume. Escaping more balls of fire and some floating black shapes, they formed a circle around the green bubble. After a few more calls of instructions from Harlume, they all charged toward the ball.

Aaden held his breath as they were about to hit it, deciding not to close his eyes. He was very relieved as he watched it quickly disappear, leaving Drakint floating in the air—just him and the Sword of Puomes. All together, the baby dragons turned around and chased the ghouls away. Harlume stuck out her sharp talons, seized the sword, and dropped it. As the group stared up into the air waiting for the sword to reach the clearing, Harlume wrapped her legs around Drakint as he began falling from the sky.

Everyone was back on a dragon again, Fhriler had the Sword of Puomes, and Harlume had trapped Drakint under his wing. The group flew back up into the air, dodging fireballs from the ghouls. As soon as the ghouls saw the Sword of Puomes, they fled, leaving only Drakint to be dealt with.

Once all seven dragons and all seven members of the Aader were near Harlume's wing, and Aaden was sticking out the sword right in front of it, Harlume slowly lifted her wings. Drakint was revealed to be sitting there, his legs crossed and his eyes closed.

"*Serrensheboise!*" Frieke yelled, causing everyone besides Drakint to cover their ears. Drakint opened his eyes.

"Drakint, what should we do with you? And how do you manage to show up everywhere?" Aaden asked seriously. There was a long pause. Then Drakint, tears flowing, shook his head, seeming too full of emotion to speak.

"Are you still with Grutch?" Cedar asked.

Still crying, Drakint said, "No, I've just escaped from a prison there. I don't know what happened to me. I was overcome with greed for riches and power. I was a different person, an evil person. The last time I remember feeling like myself was when I was helping the island people. I went into a mysterious cave to look for a source of fresh water. It seemed like I must have blacked out or something. The next thing I remember is being in Grutch, presenting a plan to bring troops to the Northern Woods to obtain gold and powerful metals."

Aaden and his friends looked at each other, some with more skepticism than others. But to Aaden, it seemed that Drakint was sincere, that something evil had been in the cave with Drakint and taken control of him. Perhaps Frieke's spell had pushed out the evil presence.

"Do you want to join us?" Aaden said. Rederin, Cedar, and Faten looked at him with great surprise.

"Why are you asking me that, Aaden? You know I betrayed you," Drakint said.

"We started out on this quest together. We...I trust you. It wasn't really you doing all those awful things," Aaden said. He knew he was taking a risk, and he crossed his fingers behind his back, hoping that it would work.

"I can't. It just wouldn't be right. And look, you don't need me. You have them," Drakint replied sadly.

"Drakint, we've learned that we need each other, that together we're much more than we are separately. We were lucky to be here, to have survived and learned so much. We should give you the benefit of the doubt. If we turn you away, you might not survive. Anyway, we have a lot of catching up to do. How in the world did you manage to arrive to foil us everywhere we went?" Aaden said. Out of the corner of his eye, he could see the others nodding, convinced they should give Drakint a chance. All except for Mr. Ponn, who looked very tense, and was holding his face in his hands.

Drakint walked closer to Aaden and held out his hand. Aaden took it.

"I never dreamed you guys would give me another chance," he said.

The Oath of the Aader

I, a loyal member and follower of the Aader,

Solemnly swear

That wherever the Aader go,

Whenever they do something,

And however they do it,

I will follow and not complain.

I, a loyal member and follower of the Aader,

Solemnly swear

That whatever the Aader do,

Whenever the Aader do it,

I will not ever

Abandon the Aader in any way.

I, a loyal member and follower of the Aader,

Solemnly swear

That I will always, always do

Whatever it takes to

Help the Aader

In any way possible.

I, a loyal member and follower of the Aader,

Hereby pledge my life to the Aader,

And if I needed to,

For the sake of the Aader,

I would take my own life,

For without the Aader, I would not have a life worth living.

Finished on May 2.

This oath was written by Cedar shortly after Drakint rejoined the Aader.

About the Author

Brian Wong is a fifth grader at Otis Elementary School and resides with his family in Alameda, California. He began writing his debut novel, The Aader, shortly after winning first place in a local writing contest in fourth grade. He is now at work on The Equinox, the second book in the Dragondaire Trilogy. He types his own manuscripts and designed the illustrations and the cover for The Aader.

978-0-595-36910-2
0-595-36910-3

Printed in the United States
47275LVS00003B/160-210